AMISH FAVOR

AMISH BED AND BREAKFAST BOOK 3

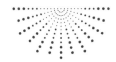

RUTH HARTZLER

Amish
ROMANCE BOOKS

Amish Favor (Amish Bed and Breakfast, Book 3)
Amish Romance
Copyright © 2017 by Ruth Hartzler
All Rights Reserved
ISBN 9781925689129

———

Scripture quotations are from The Holy Bible, English Standard Version® (ESV®), copyright © 2001 by Crossway, a publishing ministry of Good News Publishers. Used by permission. All rights reserved.

———

*P*ennsylvania Dutch is a dialect. It is often written as it sounds, which is why you will see the same word written several different ways. The word 'Dutch' has nothing to do with Holland, but rather is likely a corruption of the German word 'Deitsch' or 'Deutsch'.

Glossary

ab im kopp - addled in the head
Ach! (also, *Ack!*) - Oh!
aenti - aunt
appeditlich - delicious
Ausbund - Amish hymn book
bedauerlich - sad

bloobier - blueberry

boppli - baby

bopplin - babies

bro - bread

bruder(s) - brother(s)

bu - boy

Budget, The - weekly newspaper for Amish and Mennonite communities. Based on Sugarcreek, Ohio, and has 2 versions, Local and National.

buwe - boys

daag - day

Daed, Datt, Dat (vocative) - Dad

Diary, The - Lancaster County based Amish newspaper. Focus is on Old Order Amish.

Dawdi (also, *Daadi*) (vocative) - Grandfather

dawdi haus (also, *daadi haus*, *grossdawdi haus*) - grandfather's or grandparents' house (often a small house behind the main house)

de Bo - boyfriend

Die Botschaft - Amish weekly newspaper. Based in PA but its focus is nation-wide.

demut - humility

denki (or *danki*) - thank you

Der Herr - The Lord

dochder - daughter

dokter - doctor

doplich - clumsy

dumm - dumb

dummkopf - idiot, dummy

Dutch Blitz - Amish card game

English (or *Englisch*) (adjective) - A non-Amish person

Englischer (noun) - A non-Amish person

familye - family

ferhoodled - foolish, crazy

fraa - wife, woman

froh - happy

freind - friend

freinden - friends

gegisch - silly

geh - go

gern gheschen (also, gern *gschehne*) - you're welcome

Gott (also, *Gotte*) - God

grank - sick, ill

grossboppli - grandbaby

grossdawdi (also, *dawdi, daadi haus, gross dawdi*) - grandfather, or, in some communities, great grandfather

grosskinskind - great-grandchild

grosskinskinner - great-grandchildren

grossmammi (or *grossmudder*) - grandmother

gross-sohn - grandson

grossvadder - grandfather (see also *grossdawdi*)

gude mariye - good morning

guten nacht (also, *gut nacht*) - good night

gude nochmiddaag - good afternoon

gut - good

haus - house

Herr - Mr.

Hiya - Hi

hochmut - pride

Hullo (also, *Hallo*) - Hello

hungerich - hungry

Ich liebe dich - I love you

jah (also *ya*) - yes

kaffi (also, *kaffee*) - coffee

kapp - prayer covering worn by women

kichli - cookie

kichlin - cookies

kinn (also, *kind*) - child

kinner - children

kinskinner - Grandchildren

Kumme (or *Kumm*) - Come

lieb - love, sweetheart

liewe - a term of endearment, dear, love

liede - song

maid (also, *maed*) - girls

maidel (also, *maedel*) - girl

Mamm (also, *Mammi*) - Mother, Mom

Mammi - Grandmother

mann - man

mariye-esse - breakfast

mei - my

meidung - shunning

mei lieb - my love

mein liewe - my dear, my love

menner - men

mudder - mother

naerfich - nervous

naut (also, *nacht*) - night

nee (also *nein*) - no

nix - nothing

nohma - name

onkel - uncle

Ordnung - "Order", the unwritten Amish set of rules, different in each community

piffle (also, *piddle*) - to waste time or kill time

Plain - referring to the Amish way of life

rett (also, *redd*) - to put (items) away or to clean up.

rootsh (also, *ruch*) - not being able to sit still.

rumspringa (also, *rumschpringe*) - Running around years - when Amish youth (usually around the age of sixteen) leave the community for time and can be

English, and decide whether to commit to the Amish way of life and be baptized.

schatzi - honey

schee - pretty, handsome

schecklich - scary

schmaert - smart

schtupp - family room

schweschder - sister

schweschdern - sisters

schwoger - brother-in-law

seltsam - strange, unnatural

sohn - son

vadder - father

verboten - forbidden

Vorsinger - Song leader

was its let - what is the matter?

wie gehts - how are you?

wilkum (also, *wilkom*) - welcome

wunderbar (also, *wunderbaar*) - wonderful

yer - you

yourself - yourself

youngie (also, *young)* - the youth

yung - young

CHAPTER 1

Tiffany

*E*than stretched out his hand for the boat. The boat was small and sturdy, and carved from wood by his father. Every afternoon, when the men worked in the fields and the women sewed, Ethan and Tiffany scampered down to the river's edge to race their boats and to splash their small fingers into the current, taking care not to wet their clothes.

Looking back, Tiffany was never sure when she first realized Ethan was not like the rest of her world. His world was not made of big red buses like the ones she rode in England when visiting her grandmother, but a world made of horses and buggies. Sometimes Tiffany would stand and watch the men in the field and the women in their unusual clothes, but that always made Ethan sulk, for all he wanted to do was play.

After all, the sight of a horse and buggy was not unusual to Ethan.

When Ethan's father heard about Tiffany, he had made her a little wooden boat of her very own. Now, with her head pressed against the cool glass of the airplane window and a packet of stale peanuts in her lap, she wondered where that boat was now. Was she not fast enough to snatch it from the current one early fall afternoon? Did that little wooden boat sail away, tossed upon a shore far away from her parents' Bed and Breakfast?

Tiffany turned off her cell phone and daydreamed while the plane moved down the tarmac. Goodbye to rainy old England. She'd only been in England for the summer, but it had felt like a lifetime. For some reason, the cobbled streets and gray skies had brought back so many memories of Ethan, their river, and their boats.

Where was Ethan now? Did he work in the fields like all those men she used to see? Was he married to one of those women in their unusual clothes? Did he have children? If he did, she wondered if he made them wooden boats, like his father before him, and his father before him.

Once upon a time, it might have been their children he would have made a boat for, Ethan and Tiffany's. Their children might be stretching out on the warm grass right now, and she watching them.

Now the woman next to her stretched and settled down for the flight. Tiffany reminded herself not to drink too much water, because she didn't want to need to use the bathroom and have to move past the woman. Tiffany wasn't one for crowds or public places. To stop the woman getting too comfortable, Tiffany stuck her elbow in the woman's side. The woman squealed, sending her water bottle flying in front of a flight attendant. Tiffany rolled her eyes as glares from the other passengers followed.

Nine hours later, the plane would land in LA. Tiffany only half paid attention to the safety instructions as she was thinking of home. Her mother was the type to put her oxygen mask on and not think of anyone else, but Tiffany knew Ethan would have worried about all those around him.

She had such a strong idea of him, even though

they had not seen each other since they were children, drinking lemonade underneath the trees that glistened in the yellow sunlight. They used to wander unnoticed into the kitchen of the Bed and Breakfast to eat candy and chocolate cake. Sometimes, Tiffany would read books to Ethan, their small feet dangling over the back steps of the porch.

Tiffany was not sure when they outgrew their childhood games, or when she and Ethan stopped racing their boats down by the river. One summer, she went to visit her grandmother for her annual trip to England, and when she returned, there was no Ethan and Tiffany. There was Tiffany, but then there was no Ethan. Or was there? She had not seen him for so many years now. Was his hair still the color of wheat? Were his eyes the color of the forget-me-not flowers that grew on the side of the road?

As the plane rose into the heavens, she wondered if she would recognize him now. She wondered if he would even recognize her. She had been such a wild little girl, always climbing trees and playing football. One year she broke her arm three times at school. The children had teased her about her wildness, and they had also teased her about her looks, but she had grown beautiful since, a lovely-looking young woman with long blonde hair. Her parents had even paid a fortune to have her teeth fixed so she wouldn't be an embarrassment to them. No, she did not think Ethan would recognize her.

Her grandmother called her an English Rose, though she was not English at all. Reclining in her seat, Tiffany considered that she would miss her grandmother. Her grandmother was far more kindly than her uptight mother. Her grandmother liked a neat house, but she had always understood that children are children, and sometimes milk will be spilled and knees grazed. Tiffany's mother had never understood that.

Tiffany sighed. If only she could live with her grandmother in England, take High Tea every Sunday and read about the Royal family in those melodramatic tabloids they have in all the grocery stores.

Maybe she could return next summer and marry a British man? That would make her grandmother very happy, and her mother very unhappy. The thought gave Tiffany chills of pleasure, and she sank back happily into her seat to drink her soda and watch the sunlight play off the clouds.

All of a sudden she stiffened, and her mouth went dry. To stop the feeling of being strangled, she unzipped her hoodie and took several calming breaths. She remembered now what happened to the little wooden boat she used to race with Ethan down by the river all those fall afternoons ago.

Her mother had thrown it in the trash.

CHAPTER 2

Miriam

---

*A*s the bright sun hung high in the late morning sky, Miriam looked out over the fields. Such beauty and peace were apparent on the outside, but inside, she was struggling with a decision. She had been short-handed enough at the Bed and Breakfast before, but now things seemed even more desperate.

Miriam sipped her meadow tea and glanced over at Jonas, who was seated next to her on the steps of the porch.

"What's wrong, Miriam?" he asked, a concerned expression on his face.

Miriam looked down at her cup of tea and sighed. "It's just that I'm down my only full-time worker now, since Martha and James got married. I'm happy for them both, really I am, but it just puts me further in a bind. I can't even ask my own *dochder*, Rachel, to come back to work, because she and Isaac recently had a *boppli*."

"Well, it's an unfortunate situation for the business, but you can't let that get you down. At least Rachel and Martha had to leave for good reasons rather than bad." Jonas looked over at her, his face gentle. "Miriam, you're a *grossmammi* now. That's reason enough to be excited! You'll find another to take Martha's place. I'm sure of it."

Miriam was enjoying being a new *grossmammi*, but the stress of running and renovating the B&B was taking its toll. It had been such a long, difficult journey thus far, but up to now, she had been making things work and had managed to overcome all the obstacles that had befallen her. She knew she couldn't give up just yet. Maybe Jonas was right; perhaps she would find a new employee soon.

"I just don't know who to ask," she sighed, looking at her meadow tea once more. She set down her cup and turned to Jonas. "I think I'll go out into the garden. It's so beautiful out today; it might help me clear my mind a little before trying to figure out how to replace Martha."

"Of course." Jonas stood up without hesitation. He fixed his hat and then offered his hand to Miriam to help her to her feet. She smiled happily for a moment, almost losing herself in his eyes. No matter how many people moved away, there was still one person who she was happy to have nearby.

Miriam nodded and motioned for Jonas to follow. She stopped at the edge of the garden and admired the beauty of the scenery. The multitude of colors from the flowers blended seamlessly with the greens of the vegetables, almost as if someone had painted a portrait under the pastel sky. "Look how lovely the property is," she said, spinning around and admiring the vast fields and small hills. "Too bad once we go back inside it'll be all back to worrying about the business again."

Jonas turned to her. He spoke in a soft, sincere tone. "Miriam, I've yet to see you go up against something that you couldn't overcome, so let this be one of those things. Besides, you're not alone," he said, smiling.

"But that's the problem." Miriam sighed. "As far

as running and operating the B&B, I *am* alone. You and your crew have been wonderful, but I still need help doing things around the place like cooking, cleaning, and tending to guests." She looked back out over the garden and exhaled.

"Are there no girls in the community who need a job?" Jonas asked.

Miriam shook her head. "All of them are already employed, except one."

"So why not hire her to help you?"

Miriam started to walk again, this time away from the garden and toward the creek. Jonas followed by, always staying close to her side. "Well, she's just very young and silly. I don't know how the guests would take to such a girl, so I'm very hesitant."

"Hesitant enough to do all of that work by yourself instead?" Jonas asked.

Miriam adjusted her bonnet. "Not really, but I need someone who can work full time and is willing to live here," she said. The pair continued walking through the fields until they came upon the river. Miriam stepped into the gazebo and took a seat, looking out over the water.

Jonas followed and sat beside her. He let his hands fall into his lap. "Imagine waking up to this view every day. What better bonus for an employee?" Jonas smiled as he continued to watch the stream.

Miriam wasn't quite sure how to word her next statement, but she knew it was her only hope. If there were no Amish girls in the community who could work for her full-time, the only alternative was to hire someone from outside the community. She glanced over at Jonas and tried to speak, but the words just wouldn't escape her lips. After struggling with her thoughts, she finally spoke. "I was actually thinking my best hope is to hire an *Englischer*. I would imagine there are plenty of girls in the town who need a job."

Jonas frowned. "Miriam, are you sure about this? Don't you remember what happened with Amos?"

Miriam paused for a moment, apprehension welling up within her. No, she wouldn't give into the fear. "*Nee*, not all *Englischer*s are good, as we unfortunately had to witness firsthand with Amos, but not all of them are bad either. I've met plenty of *Englischers* who have respect for and show courtesy to others. It's just a matter of finding the right girl for the job."

"I suppose you're right in that regard, Miriam,

but it's still somewhat of an unsettling prospect, given what happened before. I thought Amos was a fine upstanding young *mann* who would never turn out to be who he really was. I'm not saying they're bad, not even in the slightest. All I'm saying is that you have to be careful trusting outsiders sometimes, as shameful as it might be to say." Jonas looked back out over the creek. "I've been able to trust James completely since the day I first met him. I never once had a doubt about the kind of man he was, and I have yet to doubt him since. And look at Ethan. He's only been on the job for a short time since his *familye* returned to town, but there hasn't been a single issue. And the very reason for that is that they are Amish *menner*, so there's no cause for concern." He looked back at Miriam, and she could see the sadness behind his eyes. "I don't want to see you go through what you did with Amos again. I already blame myself for that."

A churning feeling lodged in the pit of Miriam's stomach. This time, however, it wasn't a pleasant feeling. It was more like regret or remorse, feelings she didn't usually experience. She didn't like seeing Jonas so worried and remorseful, especially when he had done nothing wrong. She took a deep breath and tried to reassure Jonas that he wasn't to blame.

"You should never place blame on yourself for such a thing. What happened with Amos wasn't your fault in any sense of the word. If anything, you were a large part of the reason we stopped him," she said with a smile. "You're part of the reason that Eden is still operating as a Bed and Breakfast, and it's only improving as the days pass by."

Jonas seemed reluctant to believe her. He let out a long sigh. "*Jah*, you're right, but it'll only keep improving as long as we can trust those around us."

"Jonas, you just have to forgive Amos for his misdeeds and let it go. I know it can be tough, but it's something we have to do. If we hold onto resentment and fear of the people we interact with, doesn't that make us similar to those we're afraid of?" Miriam asked.

He looked down at his hands as they continued to rest in his lap. "I do forgive him," he said calmly. "I harbor no ill will against Amos, or anyone else for that matter. What I struggle with is this: the person who caused so much trouble around here only had the opportunity to do so because of me. I brought him here," Jonas said.

Miriam frowned. "Well, in that case, I invited you and your crew here, so am I at fault as well?"

Jonas stood up. He didn't speak right away, but

Miriam could almost predict his next response. "Of course not. I would never say such a thing, but…"

"You can't blame yourself for those things either, then," she said. "It was an unfortunate series of events caused by a troubled young man who made some mistakes. For all we know, he might now regret ever causing trouble. He was just so caught up with the idea of finding the lost treasure that he made some poor decisions." Miriam climbed down the few steps of the gazebo and motioned for Jonas to walk back with her. "As long as the new employee of mine doesn't believe in the legends of hidden treasure, there shouldn't be any problems that I can't handle."

They walked together back toward the *haus*, chatting about happier things, like James and Martha. "Ever since we started working here I could tell James was becoming protective of Martha," Jonas said, "but I didn't expect things to work out so well for them both. Take a good look at him when you see him around the B&B now. He just seems very thankful for everything he's been given, even more so than before, and that's saying a lot. His *baard* is even starting to grow in now," he said with a laugh.

As they passed by the garden, Miriam looked up at the sun, which was now closer to the center of the sky. "We should probably both get back to work," she said.

"*Jah*, we should. I have some walls to get finished and you have a new employee to find and hire." Jonas looked over at Miriam with a wide smile. "*Denki* for the talk. It started out as me trying to help you through your worries, but you ended up helping me out instead."

Miriam thought about his words carefully for what seemed like an eternity. She felt like he was someone that she needed in her life, but the thought still frightened her a little. They had grown to become *gut* friends, and she didn't want to lose that, no matter what it took to hold onto him. "Jonas, you help me out without even trying to." She smiled and gestured toward the B&B. "How about we turn this day around, for both of our sakes?"

Jonas nodded. "That sounds like a *gut* plan. The *menner* and I will be working upstairs today mostly, but if you need anything at all, please just give us a shout." They walked up to the front door and paused, looking at each other one last time before entering.

Miriam smiled at him. "Jonas, *denki* again. I was afraid such a beautiful day would be ruined by my concerns, but once again, you were there to help me through it."

CHAPTER 3

Miriam

*J*onas had left to speak to his workers, James, Martha's new husband, and his new worker, Ethan.

Miriam sat at the table in her large kitchen, her pen hovering over a piece of paper. She looked at the five crumpled pieces of paper that sat beside her.

Surely it shouldn't be so hard to write an advertisement for an assistant? Still, it was the first time she had to do such a thing. Normally, she would just ask the Bishop for his advice. In fact, she had done precisely that, and it was he who had suggested she hire an *Englischer*. He said there were no suitable girls within the community.

The memory of Amos, the last *Englischer* who had worked at Eden, was still fresh in her mind. It was not long ago that Amos had been taken away by the police and charged. Still, she knew not all *Englischers* were like that.

Miriam set her pen down and rubbed her throbbing temples. Why was she having such trouble coming up with something? Maybe should she should ask Jonas. She shook her head. *Nee*, that was a bad idea. Jonas had his hands full with his new employee, Amos's replacement, Ethan. Ethan was a tall, gentle *mann* from the community and Jonas said he would make a good carpenter.

Miriam sighed and stood up. Maybe it was time to make some more meadow tea, anything to procrastinate.

The roar of an engine brought her to her feet.

Miriam hurried outside, and gasped with shock when she saw Mrs. Bedshill's car. Debra Bedshill was a particularly unpleasant woman who had made life most difficult for Miriam when she had first moved to town. Debra Bedshill and her husband, Clark, owned a rival B&B in town and had all but threatened Miriam when she had tried to start the business at Eden. In fact, they had made it very difficult for Miriam to hire any workers at all.

Miriam could feel her heart beating out of her chest. What did Debra Bedshill want now? More threats? She looked around for Jonas, but he was nowhere to be seen. And he wasn't her husband; he was her builder. *Nee*, she had to handle this by herself.

Miriam took a deep breath and walked down to the front gate. Debra Bedshill was already out of her car, leaning against it with one arm, the fingers of her other hand drumming impatiently on the car roof.

CHAPTER 4

Miriam

"Good morning, Mrs. Bedshill."

"Good morning, Mrs. Berkholder."
Debra Bedshill continued to drum her fingers, and glared at Miriam. Miriam again wondered why the woman was there—was it to threaten her again? She wiped her sweaty palms on her apron. "What can I do for you, Mrs. Bedshill?"

"I have an important matter to speak to you about."

Mrs. Bedshill did not continue talking, so

Miriam was at a loss. She walked closer to the car, but Mrs. Bedshill's fidgeting increased.

"Would you care to come inside for a cup of tea?"

Mrs. Bedshill looked horrified, as if Miriam had offered her a venomous snake. "No, that won't be necessary." She hesitated, and then licked her lips. "I've just come to ask you a favor."

"A favor?" Miriam was taken aback. Surely this had to be a trick; what favor could Mrs. Bedshill possibly ask of her? A horrible, sinking feeling lodged in the pit of her stomach. Finally, she found her voice. "What sort of favor?" She was dismayed to hear her voice catch as she spoke.

"It's about my daughter, Tiffany."

Miriam frowned. Mrs. Bedshill was here to ask her a favor, a favor about her daughter, Tiffany? She didn't even know that Debra and Clark Bedshill had a daughter.

Debra was still talking. "Tiffany is my only daughter. She's in serious danger of being disinherited by my husband, and last week she wrecked her car. We had to buy her a new one. She's just returned from her annual vacation in England with her grandmother. Each year she returns more unruly and undisciplined than the year before."

"I'm sorry to hear that," Miriam said politely, wondering what this all had to do with her.

Debra Bedshill stopped drumming her fingernails and took a step toward Miriam. "Tiffany is generally developing into an intolerable brat. Now, word around town is that your place is well run and organized, despite my previous misgivings." She avoided Miriam's gaze as she said it. "I imagine it's a place where a young woman could learn structure and discipline, even a daughter as spoiled as my own. I've come here to ask you to take my daughter to work for you."

Miriam sputtered. Her mind raced. Sure, she wanted a new worker at the B&B, and in fact had been trying to compose an advertisement at that very moment, but surely she couldn't take on Debra Bedshill's daughter, a daughter who by her mother's own admission was intolerable and spoiled.

"Mind you, my daughter isn't trained for anything, so I'll pay you."

"You'll pay me?" Miriam said in shock.

Mrs. Bedshill nodded. "Yes. I can hardly ask you to pay an unskilled young woman, a young woman who is likely to give you quite some trouble.

In fact, not only will I pay you to take her on, but I might be tempted to make a small outlay toward the B&B's future if you can manage to hammer the girl into shape in the process."

Miriam did not know what to say. "Um, um," was all she could force from her mouth. A spoiled girl, at her well-run establishment? What if she was rude to the guests? This might not be a solution at all. And furthermore, it might be a trick. Debra and her husband, Clark, had made no secret of the fact that they did not want Eden to succeed. What if this was a ploy to bring Eden down? This could all be some sort of a trick, a ruse. Miriam was never good at thinking on her feet, and right now she had no ready reply. "I'll certainly think it over," she said honestly.

Debra Bedshill's face turned beet red. "No, that's not part of the bargain. Either you agree now, or I'll go elsewhere." She crossed her arms over her chest.

Miriam made up her mind on the spot. She did need an assistant, and while she didn't actually need the goodwill of the Bedshills, it certainly wouldn't hurt to have it. They had stopped tradespersons attending Eden in the past and had caused her no end of trouble. Perhaps this would be the solution. She only hoped it wasn't a trick. "All right then. I agree, but please ask your daughter not to be rude to guests or be in any way disruptive."

Debra Bedshill snorted rudely. "That will be *your* problem, Mrs. Berkholder. The girl *is* unruly. Don't say you haven't been warned." She reached into her purse and pulled out a handful of notes which she shoved into Miriam's hand. "A gesture of goodwill. I didn't want to come to you, but I thought you people might be able to do some good for the girl, because nothing else has worked."

With that, she jumped into her large car and sped away with a squeal of tires.

Miriam stood there watching after her. She was shocked and did not know what to make of the situation.

"Was that Mrs. Bedshill?"

Miriam spun around to see Jonas standing behind her. "Yes. She…"

Jonas interrupted her. "She didn't threaten you again, did she?"

Miriam shook her head. "*Nee*, she came to ask me a favor."

"A favor?" Jonas asked. He frowned so deeply that deep lines formed at the side of his eyes.

Miriam nodded. "*Jah*, it was the strangest thing. Did you know she has a daughter called Tiffany?"

Jonas shook his head. "*Nee*, I didn't know they had any children, but then I don't know the townspeople, only the ones I work for. So she asked you a favor about her daughter?"

"She said her *dochder* is spoiled and out of control and she wants to send her here to work for me."

Jonas's jaw dropped in shock. "I can't believe it! What did you say?"

"I didn't know what to think at first, but I *am* looking for an assistant, as we discussed. What's more, Debra Bedshill offered to pay me to take the girl on. I wanted to think it over, but she insisted that I made the decision on the spot. I agreed to take her on."

Jonas's eyes grew wider. "You did?"

Miriam could see he wanted to say something more, but he chose to remain silent. Miriam clutched herself. "*Jah*, and I don't know if I did the right thing. I'm never very *gut* at thinking on my feet. Still, I'd been praying for the right person to come and this could be an answer from *Gott*."

Jonas raised his eyebrows, and Miriam could see he didn't agree with her, but he was too polite to say so. She pressed on. "What harm can it do? She's going to pay me to have her daughter working here, and it might do the girl some good."

"I only hope it isn't some sort of a trap to ruin your business," Jonas said.

That was exactly what Miriam was thinking.

CHAPTER 5

Miriam

*T*he next morning, Miriam was sweeping the porch, when a flashy sports car slid sideways to a stop. A tall, thin young woman wearing rather too-tight clothes and high heels slowly got out of the car, chewing gum with her mouth open and texting on her phone. Miriam was at once horrified. In all her imagination, she hadn't thought the girl could be this bad. The girl marched over to Miriam.

"You must be Tiffany," Miriam said. "I'm Mrs. Berkholder. You may call me Miriam."

"Please show me to my room," Tiffany said in an imperious manner, rolling the gum around in her mouth. "Send for the help to come and get my bags from my car."

"You're here to work for me," Miriam said in a tone that brooked no nonsense. "You *are* the help now. You will take your own bags to your room, and I will confiscate your phone."

The young woman's mouth fell open, and she muttered some rather rude words under her breath.

"There'll be none of that language around here," Miriam said firmly. "I hope the two of us can get along fine, but that entirely depends on your attitude. I'll let you settle in for the day, and then tomorrow morning you can start work. We start work here at five. Now, I'll need the keys to your car."

The girl threw her phone and her keys in the dirt at Miriam's feet and then stormed over to the car to get her bags. Miriam resisted the urge to roll her eyes. What on earth had she gotten herself into? Had she been wrong in thinking this was *Gott's* plan? She watched as the angry Tiffany sullenly unpacked her bags from the car and then struggled with them to the porch. What on earth did the girl have in those bags?

Miriam let out one long sigh and then followed Tiffany to the front door which she opened for her. "Follow me," she said to Tiffany.

Normally, Miriam would have helped Tiffany with her bags, but the girl was so unruly and undisciplined that Miriam thought it better that she do it herself. She showed Tiffany to a small bedroom.

"Is this my room?" Tiffany said in horror. "It's disgusting! Where's the TV?"

Miriam's words caught in her throat. While the room was small, she thought it rather pleasant and sufficient. It had everything one needed, a beautiful handmade quilt over a double bed which had a sturdy bed frame, and a large mahogany dresser stood against the wall.

The quilt was a Wholecloth, Feathered Pineapple Quilt. The thin batting showed off the fine quilting, and the back of the quilt was covered with the same white cotton muslin as the front. Miriam did not expect that Tiffany would appreciate the traditional quilt, but she was shocked at the way she was so rudely dismissive of the room. Why, there was even a large closet for guests to hang their clothes. And while there was only one small window, it nevertheless afforded a beautiful view of the landscape stretching out to the far hills.

Miriam finally found her voice. "You're living here as one of the workers, not as a guest," she said evenly. "We don't have TV, and your mother thought it would be good for you to live as the Amish." Miriam sent up a silent prayer to *Gott* for forgiveness for the exaggeration.

"What's your internet password?" Tiffany asked belligerently. "Surely the guests have internet!"

"We'll see about that later," Miriam said. "We Amish don't use the internet either."

Tiffany shot her a defiant look. "I know you people do use it for business."

Miriam crossed her arms. "Well, when you're working nicely in the business, we will see about you using the internet. Right now I suggest you unpack your bags and get some rest. Dinner will be at six this evening. Tonight I'll be providing dinner for the guests and eating with them, but that isn't usually the case. You're welcome to join us, but I ask you not to be disruptive."

Tiffany took off her heels and threw them dramatically to the floor. "Of course I won't be disruptive! What sort of a person do you think I am?" She pouted.

Miriam chose to ignore her outburst. "When you're settled, I'll show you around the property. You can find me in the kitchen."

With that, Miriam walked downstairs. She needed some peppermint tea to dispel the headache that was rapidly forming, but right now, she was going to lock the girl's car keys and her phone in the safe.

TIFFANY WAS FURIOUS. As soon as the awful Amish woman shut the door, Tiffany picked up her shoes and tossed them at the door. She held her breath, half expecting the woman to return, but luckily she didn't.

Tiffany flung herself on her bed and burst into tears. How could her mother do this to her? There was no internet, and she didn't even have her cell phone. What sort of a place was this? It was just like being in prison, and a labor camp at that! And all she had done was wreck her car and answer her mother back. Yet, for something as insignificant as that, her parents had threatened to cut off her allowance if she did not stay with this dreadful Amish person.

With that in mind, she stopped sobbing and reached for the lamp near her bed. It switched on, and Tiffany heaved a sigh of relief. She knew that Amish people didn't have electricity or phones. Still, she knew enough about the Amish to know that a Bed and Breakfast would have amenities.

CHAPTER 6

Miriam

---

*M*iriam wasn't looking forward to dinner that night, not with Tiffany being there. Who knew what the girl was likely to do? It certainly wouldn't go over well if she had a tantrum in front of the guests.

Simon Gibson was a history major writing a book on the history of the area. He said he was freelance, that he was recently sacked from a big paper and was looking for a big story. Miriam didn't quite trust him. She was concerned he was there looking for Captain Kidd's treasure. And then there was Delia Wilson, a newly divorced woman. If Miriam were to be unkind, she would say that Delia was a mean and cranky woman. Of course, Miriam kept those thoughts to herself. Delia talked about nothing else except her ex-husband, Frank, who was the worst person in the world if Delia could be believed.

And then there was the retired couple, Phyllis and Murray Woods. They were always secretive and uptight. All Miriam knew about them was that they were in town to meet a long lost relative. They told her they had known each other when young and then had gone their separate ways, met again and then married in recent times. There was something not quite up-front about them, but she couldn't put her finger on it.

Miriam had made the whole dinner by herself, and that had made her think once more of an assistant. She didn't hold out much hope that Tiffany would prove to be an able assistant. In fact, she was sure that the young woman would have no idea how to peel a potato. Had Tiffany ever gotten her hands dirty in her entire life? Miriam did not think so.

Miriam had gone to some trouble to prepare the meal. *Englischer* guests came to her B&B to be treated to a true Amish experience, and she was always careful to give them just that. As she walked in with a large tray, she saw Tiffany sitting at the table with the other guests. Miriam breathed a sigh of relief. So far so good. Tiffany was minding her manners, even looking quite demure. She was wearing enough make-up to appear as a clown in a circus, but Miriam did not mind that. So long as Tiffany did not make a scene, Miriam would be happy.

The other guests were engaged in conversation, but Tiffany was sitting still, staring silently at her empty plate. Miriam laid one heavy container on the table and then sat down.

"What's that?" Tiffany said, rather too loudly.

"It's pot pie," Miriam said. "It's a typical Amish dish that you'll find in Lancaster County." Tiffany's face screwed up with disgust. Miriam pressed on. "It's square noodles made with chicken and gravy, and I've added various vegetables including potatoes."

"It looks like chicken and dumplings," Simon said.

"Yes, that's right," Miriam said.

"Where did its name come from?" Delia asked.

"The Pennsylvania Dutch name for the square noodles is *bot boi* which sounds a lot like pot pie."

Delia nodded. "Yes, when my horrible ex-husband Frank and I used to visit Lancaster County, we often stayed at Amish B&Bs and one time I saw a lady roll out the dough and hang it in strips to dry, right on the backs of the kitchen chairs."

Tiffany snorted rudely. "That doesn't sound hygienic!"

Delia ignored her. "Frank used to love pot pie, but then again Frank used to like anything that I didn't bake. That man was never grateful for anything I did for him. I worked my fingers to the bone for him, cooking and cleaning. I gave up my own career to put him through college. He was ungrateful. Why, he was a…" Her face flushed beet red.

Miriam thought it time to change the subject. "Simon, how's your story coming along?"

Tiffany fixed him with a look. "What story? Are you writing about the treasure here?"

"There *is* no treasure here," Miriam said firmly. "So many people have looked for it and have come up empty."

"That's not what I've heard," Tiffany said snarkily. "Everyone in town knows that Captain Kidd's treasure is buried in these parts, probably somewhere under Eden itself. Everyone knows that Eden was named after one of Captain Kidd's men, a man called Dr. John Eden. He retired to Pennsylvania and built a house in this part of town and stored his treasure here. Treasure hunters always come here looking for the lost gold."

"And of course they have never found it," Miriam said. "If there *was* any treasure here, then it would have been found by now."

Tiffany had apparently lost interest in the conversation. "I can't eat this. It's not the sort of food I'm used to. I can't even wash it down with wine, as there isn't any. What's the dessert?"

Miriam took a deep breath before answering. "Shoo fly pie. It's very sweet, with molasses and brown sugar, and it has a layer of crumb on top. I have done a dry bottom on this one, meaning it has a degree of crust on the bottom. If you prefer, I can make another one in the next few days with a wet bottom."

Tiffany screwed up her nose by way of response. Miriam noticed that the other guests exchanged glances. Well, it could be worse. She was expecting Tiffany to be rude, so the girl's behavior was no great surprise. She would just see to it that Tiffany was kept busy from now on and hopefully that would help her manners.

CHAPTER 7

Miriam

At precisely five the next morning, Miriam bent over Tiffany. Tiffany was in a deep sleep, snoring lightly. Miriam said Tiffany's name, quietly at first, and then more loudly. Finally, she shook Tiffany gently.

Tiffany woke up with a start. "Where am I?" She looked around the room wildly.

"You're at Eden, the Bed and Breakfast," Miriam said softly. "Hush, don't wake up the other guests. It's time to start work for the day."

"Work?" Tiffany said in shock.

Miriam could not resist a small smile. It was clear that work was a foreign concept to Tiffany. "Yes, I'm going to introduce you to the joys of manual labor. It's time to start an extensive cleaning of all the rooms."

Tiffany pulled the quilt back over her head. "No, it's too early for me. I never get up before midday. Can you come back in a few hours?"

Miriam pulled the quilt off Tiffany. "Out of bed, Tiffany, right now! We start work at five. That was the agreement with your mother. Do you want me to call her?"

The mention of Tiffany's mother removed the pout from Tiffany's face immediately. Miriam filed that away for future reference. It was good to know that Tiffany was worried that she would report her to her mother—Miriam would be able to hold that over her if necessary.

For the next hour or so, Miriam had to listen to Tiffany complaining about every little thing. She was going to ruin her manicure if she swept the floors; she was too sleep-deprived to work before midday; she would need more facials if she worked near the oven, and the list went on. Miriam was a patient person, but this girl truly tried her patience.

Miriam figured that even Job himself would have trouble working with Tiffany.

"Would you like some breakfast now, Tiffany?" Miriam asked.

"I can't eat a thing," Tiffany snapped at her. "I don't know how many times I have to tell you, but I always sleep until midday. I never eat before then, because I'm asleep." Her tone was belligerent.

Miriam sighed. "Please speak to me with respect, Tiffany. I suppose you can drink coffee?"

Miriam noticed that Tiffany's face lit up the mention of coffee. "Yes, please. Coffee would be good."

Miriam nodded. She was pleased to see that Tiffany could be polite, after all.

Miriam put on a strong pot of *kaffi* to brew. She sometimes made coffee and a big breakfast for Jonas and his workers, on those occasions when they started early. Right on time, Jonas came into the room, with James and his new worker, Ethan.

Miriam introduced Tiffany to the men, and noted that her eyes stayed on Ethan for quite some time. In fact, she seemed shocked to see him.

Jonas rubbed his hands together in delight. "My favorite, scrapple."

"What's scrapple?" Tiffany asked, her tone far more polite than usual.

"It's a mixture of cornmeal and meat, often pork scraps and trimmings combined with spices, flour and cornmeal, and then formed into a loaf. I usually cut it into three-quarter inch slices and pan fry it in butter until it forms a crust. Would you like to try some?"

Tiffany shook her head, but did not say anything derogatory this time.

"How about some eggs?" Miriam asked her. "There's oatmeal with raisins, applesauce, and cornmeal mush with ketchup as well. There's also some leftover shoo fly pie."

"What, for breakfast?" Tiffany asked.

The three men laughed at Tiffany's horrified tone. Miriam noticed once again that Tiffany stared at Ethan. "How about just eggs and coffee?" Miriam said.

Tiffany nodded. "Yes, please."

Miriam turned to Jonas. "Has that man arrived yet? Oscar Leadman? The one who was going to remove the rusted water trough from the fields?"

Jonas nodded. "Yes, he's already out there working on it."

"Perhaps I should invite him in for breakfast."

Jonas nodded. "Ethan, could you run down to the field and ask Mr. Leadman to come in?"

Ethan had only just pushed his chair back from the table to stand up, when there was a loud bang on the front door. A startled Miriam hurried to the front door, summoned by the urgency of the knocking. She flung open the door to see Oscar Leadman standing there. Without speaking, he thrust something into her hands. At first she thought he had simply handed her dirt, but then she saw five coins. "What's going on?" Jonas said over her shoulder.

"It's Captain Kidd's treasure," Oscar said in an excited tone.

Miriam shook her head. She'd had enough trouble with this so-called treasure, and a few dirty coins certainly weren't going to help the situation.

"I managed to get that heavy concrete trough half out of the ground, and then I found these coins under it," the man said excitedly. "Who knows, Captain Kidd's entire treasure might be buried there!"

Miriam was too shocked to speak, so she was grateful when Jonas stepped forward. "Now let's not jump to any conclusions," Jonas said. He held out his hand to Miriam. She deposited the coins in his hands and then wiped her own hands on her apron.

Jonas turned the coins over and then wiped them on his shirt. "They sure do look gold," he said hesitantly.

"Gold?" Everyone turned to see Tiffany, her eyes glittering. "Is it really Captain Kidd's lost treasure?" she said eagerly.

"They do look like old coins," Jonas said. He handed the now clean coins to Miriam.

She held one up to the sun. "Yes, they do look like coins and they do look like gold, but I can't really see what's on them. This does look like some sort of cross in the center, but the edges are so worn. It could be anything, really."

To her dismay, Simon Gibson arrived as if from nowhere. "May I see them?" Miriam handed him the coins, and he gasped. "These look exactly like coins from the time of Captain Kidd," he said. "Pirate coins! Are there any more?"

Oscar Leadman shrugged. "I just found these and brought them straight up to Mrs. Berkholder. I still have to remove the rest of the trough and then I'll have a look around, if that's all right with you, Mrs. Berkholder?"

Miriam nodded. "Please, I have a favor to ask

of everyone. There's been vandalism at Eden over the years, before I moved here, and after I moved here, I had trouble with looters and even a thief looking for Captain Kidd's lost treasure. I'm asking you all to refrain from telling the press. It's very important to this business and to me personally that journalists don't come here wanting to know about the treasure. It could bring more thieves, and it could bring more looters."

"But surely it would attract more business?" Simon asked, surprised.

Miriam shook her head. "No, it would be a detriment to the business. Guests come here for a quiet time, to get away from the world, not to be involved with journalists and a flurry of media thinking there's treasure here when there's not."

"But surely this might be treasure?" Oscar asked her.

Once more, Miriam was grateful that Jonas spoke. "Possibly, but if it is, I'm sure you can see why Mrs. Berkholder wants to keep this matter private. Please don't let this get any further. The last thing Mrs. Berkholder wants is journalists swarming all over this place."

Oscar looked disappointed, but went back to his work while the others returned to the kitchen table.

Miriam nervously wrung her hands. "I'll have to hurry. Tiffany and I will have to prepare the breakfast for the guests now," she said. Tiffany openly scowled at her. "I do hope Oscar doesn't alert the media," Miriam added. She didn't know Oscar well, and he was an *Englischer*, not from the community. "I wonder how we could find out if those coins are real?"

"There's a man in town, Alex Clark, who knows about these things," Jonas said. "He's an amateur archaeologist and has a store. Would you like me to take the coins to him?"

Miriam heaved a sigh of relief. "*Jah, denki*, Jonas. That would be *gut*. Now, you men stay and finish your breakfast, while Tiffany and I prepare breakfast for the guests. Tiffany, I'll cook the oatmeal, but I'll ask you to take cereal and fruit out to the dining table. I'll prepare the eggs and fried potatoes, and scrapple this time, but I'll show you how to do it so you can help me in future."

Tiffany scowled at her, but thankfully said nothing.

This is even worse than I thought it would be, Tiffany thought, retrieving cereal from the pantry. *Oh my goodness, these people are weird. Still, the view is better than I thought it would be.*

She turned again and looked at Ethan. He was tall with broad shoulders, and his bulging biceps could be seen under his shirt. He had liquid blue eyes, the color of forget-me-not flowers, and was tanned and ruggedly handsome.

She was sure she had gasped when she had heard his name, but he showed no recognition of her, and what's more, Miriam had said he was newly in town. He couldn't be *her* Ethan. At any rate, Ethan was a common enough Amish name. She pushed away her disappointment. She had not seen her Ethan since they were children, not after his family moved away.

Tiffany compared this Ethan with her own boyfriend, Cameron, and Cameron did not do well by the comparison. Not that Cameron was her boyfriend yet, but he sure wanted to be.

She had thought she liked Cameron, despite her mother's warnings that he was only after her money, but Cameron never made her heart race like Ethan had today. What a shame Ethan was Amish, and not normal like Cameron or she could have him as her boyfriend.

What a shame this Ethan was not her childhood friend.

Tiffany set about collecting the fruit and was so busy that she didn't think to complain. All she could think about was Ethan with his strong body and those lovely blue eyes. "What a shame," she kept muttering to herself when she thought no one was listening.

CHAPTER 8

Miriam

*M*iriam went about the day's work, worrying about the gold coins. Could it really be Captain Kidd's treasure? She certainly hoped not. Still, there was no time to worry as she had to keep such a close eye on Tiffany. Tiffany complained about everything that Miriam asked her to do. Miriam was exhausted but told herself that it would be better in the long run to spend time giving Tiffany instructions now.

Miriam was beginning to regret taking Tiffany on, but she had given her word, so there was no going back. Miriam had just asked Tiffany to do the washing up for the fifth time when there was a loud knock on the door. Miriam was puzzled—the front door was always open through the day with guests coming and going. People normally entered and rang the bell in the reception area. With a sinking feeling in the pit of her stomach, she hurried to the door. She blinked to see several strangers standing there, all armed with cameras. Someone stuck a microphone under her nose.

"What's going on?" Miriam asked in a small voice.

"Tell us about Captain Kidd's treasure," the man closest to her said.

A woman pushed past him. "How many coins were found?"

The rest of the voices became indistinguishable, as one person after the other shot questions at Miriam, all the time taking photographs. Miriam clutched the door post for support. Soon, Jonas came and shooed them all away. "You can't take photographs of us without our permission," he said sternly. "You're all trespassing on private property. I'll have to ask you to leave immediately."

"Can you verify that gold coins were found on the property today?" a man asked.

"That will be all," Jonas said firmly. He ushered Miriam inside and shut the door. Someone kept knocking for another minute or so and then thankfully the knocking stopped. Miriam gingerly crossed to the window and pulled the curtain aside. "What a relief; they've all gone," she said. "Who would've alerted those people?"

Jonas shrugged.

"I wonder if it was Oscar?" Miriam said.

"It wasn't me!" an angry voice said behind her.

Miriam swung around to see Tiffany standing there, her hands on her hips. "It wasn't me!" she said again, even more angrily this time.

"Well, the damage is done now," Jonas said in a conciliatory tone, but there was something about Tiffany's expression that made Miriam think that she might have been the one who had called the newspapers.

"This is very bad for business," Miriam said to Jonas. "This could scare the guests away. They're here for peace and to have the Amish experience, not to be harassed by the journalists." Her hand flew to her mouth. "The breakfast!" She hurried back to the kitchen.

Miriam was going to ask Tiffany to help, but thought the better of it. "Tiffany, would you please look out the front window and tell me if you see any cars out there, any that shouldn't be there such as cars belonging to the newspaper people?"

Tiffany sighed dramatically, but left the room. Miriam hurried into the dining room, where all the guests were seated. "I'm so sorry breakfast was delayed," she said. "One of our workers found some old coins and someone informed the newspapers that it was Captain Kidd's lost treasure. It isn't, of course," she added. "It's just a lot of sensationalist nonsense." As soon as she mentioned Captain Kidd, she regretted it, because all the guests' eyes at once lit up.

"I take it you didn't call the newspapers?" Simon Gibson said.

Miriam shook her head. "No, I didn't. I don't want people here asking questions. I have no idea who told them."

Simon helped himself to some cereal. "When did the person find the old coins?"

Miriam tapped her chin. "It was only about an hour ago. The journalists didn't waste any time getting here. I just can't think who called them," she said, more to herself.

Delia Wilson set down her fork on the table with a bang. "I didn't know anything about those coins.

Now if it had been my husband Frank, he would have called the newspapers—but only if he knew you didn't want him to, mind you. That man is as contrary as they come. If you say it's raining, he'll say it's sunny. He just has to disagree." Thankfully, she bit into an apple which stopped her speaking.

Miriam noticed that Phyllis and Murray Woods exchanged glances. She found it a little strange that they hadn't asked any questions. After all, the legend of Captain Kidd's lost treasure was well-known around these parts and the other guests seemed quite animated about the find. Just as she was thinking that, Murray spoke. "Were they gold coins?"

Miriam nodded. "Yes, how did you know?"

Murray smiled. "If it's treasure, then I thought it would have to be gold."

Miriam nodded. That made sense. But who had alerted the media? She figured it had to be either Oscar or Tiffany. The guests had all appeared surprised that coins had been found, so surely it couldn't have been any of them. Tiffany had been completely obnoxious since her arrival, and perhaps she thought that would be a good way to upset Miriam. On the other hand, Oscar had been quite excited about his find.

Miriam noticed that Tiffany was silent throughout the exchange. At least she wasn't making a scene, although from time to time her face screwed up. Clearly, she didn't like the taste of Amish food.

Tiffany did her best to chew through the disgusting food. Who in their right mind would eat scrapple? It tasted like donuts mixed with bits of bacon and then fried. She shook her head. If only she could get back to civilization. If only her mother had told her how long she would have to put up with this disgusting place, but her mother had given her no indication. For a moment, she considered doing everything that the Amish woman wanted in order to get a good report from her. If she did, her mother might allow her to come home sooner. She'd have to think on that some more.

Tiffany did her best not to spit out her food. Perhaps she did have to put on a good act here. That might get her to freedom sooner. And then there was Ethan. The Amish man was quite attractive, and not as weird as she had suspected an Amish man would be. In fact, if it wasn't for his strange clothes and his hat, he seemed like just a regular guy. Well, he didn't swear or drink, but apart from that he didn't seem any different.

Tiffany had to admit that she was attracted to him. I mean, what girl wouldn't be? He was much taller than she was, and those broad shoulders! Her knees went weak at the thought. His face was strong and his body muscled—not muscled from spending hours looking at himself in mirrors at the gym, but muscled from doing good, hard, honest work.

Tiffany laughed when she caught herself thinking like that. *Good, hard, honest work?* She was almost turning Amish. Tiffany looked up to see Phyllis and Murray staring at her. She forced a smile.

Yes, I will keep up this act, she thought.

CHAPTER 9

Miriam

*J*onas appeared in the doorway, looking flustered.

Miriam hurried over to him. "Was der schinner is letz?" *What on earth is wrong?*

"The coins!" he said. "They've been stolen!"

Miriam was shocked. "What do you mean? They've been stolen?" she echoed.

Jonas nodded. "*Jah.* I left them in the kitchen while I gave James and Ethan instructions and told them I was going to town to see Alex Clark about the coins, and when I came back they weren't there."

"Where exactly did you leave them?"

Jonas led Miriam to the kitchen and tapped his finger on the countertop. "Right here."

Miriam frowned. She was used to *menner* not being able to find things that were right under their noses. In fact, her husband had never been able to find anything in the pantry when she asked him to fetch it, if it was simply behind something else. Still, surely Jonas couldn't be mistaken about putting something on a countertop. "Did you see anyone around?"

He shook his head. "*Nee*, nobody at all."

Miriam ran through the events in her head. Tiffany had been with her, so that only left the guests. The guests were welcome to help themselves to coffee in the kitchen at any point. In fact, she thought all the guests had been in the kitchen just prior to lunch. Miriam clutched the countertop for support. This treasure had brought them no end of grief. The love of money truly was the root of all evil. "Don't tell me we have another thief here at Eden."

Jonas looked as though he were about to pat her on the shoulder and thought better of it. "Please don't distress yourself, Miriam. I'll do my best to find out where the coins are. Would you like me to call the sheriff?"

Miriam thought it over. "I suppose we do have to call the sheriff, but it won't be *gut* if he comes here and bothers the guests."

"But if a guest is a thief, then they might not stop at the coins," Jonas pointed out. "What if a thief starts stealing the other guests' possessions?"

"I suppose that's right." Miriam bit her lip. "*Jah*, call the sheriff then, Jonas, if you would, but please ask him not to upset the guests?"

Jonas smiled. "You can leave it to me, Miriam."

Miriam watched his departing back. Yes, she knew she always could depend on Jonas.

Tiffany was polishing the silverware in the dining room. She knew that Amish didn't have nice possessions like silver, so she supposed this was a show for the guests. Still, she wanted to ask Miriam about it later.

Tiffany scrubbed and scrubbed at the silver.

These stains looked old, but came off if she scrubbed hard enough. The smell of the silver polish was getting to her. Her mother employed plenty of maids so Tiffany had never smelled silver polish before. She always made it a point to be out of sight when the maids were bustling around as they always wanted to chat, and she did not want to chat with the help.

Tiffany crossed to the large window and struggled to open it. She stuck her head out and took a deep gulp of air. The fumes from the silver polish were absolutely disgusting and she couldn't bear another second of inhaling them. Then she thought of the thief. Perhaps she should shut the window, after all. Just then, she noticed someone down by where Oscar Leadman had removed the water trough. It was Simon Gibson, and he was skulking around, all the while looking over his shoulder.

Tiffany decided to abandon her polishing and go down to see what was going on. If Miriam found she wasn't there, she would just explain that the fumes were making her sick and that she had gone to investigate suspicious behavior. She would probably get in trouble anyway, but at least she would be able to breathe easily instead of breathing in those horrible fumes.

By the time Tiffany had gone to the front door of the Bed and Breakfast and then doubled back to the field with the water trough, there was no sign of Simon Gibson. Instead, Delia Wilson was there, on her hands and knees, her hands spread in the dirt.

"Mrs. Wilson!"

Delia stood up and swung around to face Tiffany, her face white. "I was just, um… I was just…" Her voice trailed away.

"I saw Mr. Gibson out here just a few moments ago," Tiffany said. "Did you see him?"

Delia's eyes darted wildly from side to side. "Simon? I think I saw him. He is not here now," she added unnecessarily.

Tiffany did not know what to say or do next. She had clearly seen Simon right where she was now standing, but yet here was Delia with no sign of Simon. Were the two of them in it together? Had one or both of them stolen the coins and now they were back looking for more? Tiffany looked down at Delia's dirty hands. "You've been digging."

Delia nodded, as a beet red flush traveled slowly up her face. "Yes, if you must know, I was looking for Captain Kidd's lost treasure. I wasn't going to keep it for myself. I hope you don't think that!" Her voice rose in pitch.

That's exactly what Tiffany did think, but she thought it best not to say so. "Did you find anything?"

Delia crossed her arms over her chest. "No."

Tiffany kept watching her. She certainly looked guilty, but why? Had she found more coins, and were they in her pockets right now? Or was she merely guilty at being caught digging in the area where the coins were found? Tiffany had no way of knowing. Tiffany narrowed her eyes, but did not know what to do next. She simply nodded and walked away.

Tiffany walked directly back to the house, but checked over her shoulder once or twice. When she saw that Delia was no longer watching her, she skirted around the edge of the house and hid behind a stately old beech tree. From there, she watched as Delia dug frantically in the ground. What was the woman up to? Simply hoping there were more coins there? Or was something more sinister going on? And where was Simon Gibson?

CHAPTER 10

Tiffany

*D*espite Tiffany's best intentions, she found herself unable to keep up her charade of doing hard work. By lunchtime, her hair and manicure were ruined and she was covered in grease and soot. What's more, she was furious with Miriam. Surely the woman had given her all the messiest, nastiest jobs in the kitchen.

Plus there was the fact that a very annoying sheriff had come and given her the third degree. He expected her to have the memory of an elephant.

How would she know who had been where at what time? All she could remember was the type of clothes they were wearing as well as their fashion accessories. She certainly hoped the sheriff didn't have her picked out as one of his suspects. She made a point of telling him she was Clark and Debra Bedshill's daughter. She noticed he was far more pleasant to her after that fact had been pointed out.

Miriam had sent Tiffany to have a break before lunch. She was sitting on the back porch thinking angry thoughts, when she saw Ethan approach. She didn't want to see Ethan right now. She was angry at Miriam, angry at her mother, and angry at the world. What's more, she felt awful, and was sure she looked and smelled awful, too. She slumped sullenly into her chair.

Ethan nodded to Tiffany, and then set about disconnecting one of the antique brass lighting sconces on the end of the porch, presumably as they were removing that part of the porch in order to redo it. Tiffany wondered why Ethan didn't speak to her. Couldn't he see she was upset? What was his problem? She wasn't used to men not paying her any attention. After all, she was incredibly good-looking. What man wouldn't want her? She cleared her throat loudly, but Ethan continued with his tools, completely ignoring her.

"Do you like working here?" she said, desperate for conversation.

Ethan shot her a quick glance before speaking. "Yes."

Tiffany narrowed her eyes. Was Ethan playing hard to get? "So what are you? A carpenter? Why are you doing electrical work?"

This time, Ethan did not even send her a sidelong glance. "It's my work. Jonas asked me to."

Tiffany pouted. "If Jonas asked you to jump off a cliff, would you?" she asked belligerently.

To her shock, Ethan burst into laughter. "Are Amish people allowed to laugh?" she asked him.

For some reason, that only made him laugh all the harder. He collected his tools, nodded to her, and walked away.

The nerve of that man! Tiffany could not believe he had treated her so rudely. Surely he couldn't be immune to her charms? Of course not —he was clearly only pretending.

The rest of the afternoon was a blur. Tiffany had broken just about every fingernail, and her make-up was streaked. Her feet were aching. She had never worked so hard in her life. In fact, she was sure she was allergic to furniture polish. If only she could find a way to call her mother and tell her that the furniture polish was making her sick. Surely her mother wouldn't force her to remain if she had a medical problem?

Tiffany was scrubbing away at the sideboard in the dining room because Miriam had told her to polish it until she could see her reflection in it. She had furniture polish stuck under her fingernails. She paused to scratch some out and sneezed violently.

At that point, she saw James and Ethan walking down the outside corridor. James continued on, but Ethan stopped. "That was a loud sneeze." He looked amused.

"I have allergies. I shouldn't be doing this," she said, hoping to gain his sympathy.

One eyebrow quirked upward. "Allergies?" he repeated. "What sort of allergies?"

"I'm allergic to furniture polish."

Ethan laughed. For some reason he seemed to find it particularly funny. "More like allergic to work." With that, he left.

Miriam picked up two empty platters from on

top of the sideboard and threw them at the spot where Ethan had just been. They missed, and shattered all over the door post. To her dismay, Miriam appeared at that very moment. Miriam did not look pleased. "What's going on here?" she said sternly.

"Ethan was rude to me. He said I was allergic to work."

Miriam shook her head. "That is absolutely no excuse to break my equipment. I'm going to tell your mother about this, and deduct it from your pay. I can't have any more displays like this, Tiffany."

Tiffany wiped her eyes. This was not going at all to plan. She had really wanted to make a good impression so she could get out of this place sooner, but things hadn't gone how she wanted. Tiffany stomped her foot. "I demand you let me out of here right now!" she wailed. "I demand you call my mother and tell her I'm sick. I can't keep working."

Miriam ignored her. "Tiffany, you're behaving like a spoiled child, but you're a grown woman. Please take time to reflect on your actions. I want you to go to your room and read this book." Miriam opened one of the cabinet drawers and produced a large, leather bound book. "Stay in your room for the rest of the afternoon and read this book," she said as she handed it to Tiffany. "It will do you some good. I know you think you have it bad, but this book will show you that there were others who had it much worse than you have it now. Read it carefully, and it will help you get perspective. And bear in mind that the health inspection is due next month. If you think polishing furniture is hard, wait until you experience having to clean a kitchen for the county health inspector."

Tiffany stormed off to her room, clutching the heavy book. She was going to toss it on her bed, but then paused. She didn't want to damage such an old and probably valuable book. Instead, she sat on the bed and looked around the room. She had her laptop, but there was no internet; there was no TV; she didn't even have her phone. What would she do without social media? She felt like she had died and gone to hell.

Tiffany looked at the book title. The *Martyrs Mirror*. Well, that certainly didn't sound like it had a happy ending. She figured it wasn't a light romance novel. Surely they provided books for guests. Tiffany poked around the room, looking in the closet, the dresser, and even under the bed, but did not even turn up a single book. "Well then, I'll have to read you," she said aloud to the book. She sat back against the solid bed head and pulled the large book onto her knees. It seemed to be written in old-fashioned English. Tiffany sighed aloud. "What else did I expect!" she said angrily.

Tiffany began to read, but was horrified to read of an eighty-seven year old man who was about to be put to death for his beliefs. She slammed the book shut, climbed off the bed, and walked over to the window. It was a lovely sunny day. If she didn't have to work, she would rather go for a walk than to be stuck in this room reading a book about people who had been put to death for their beliefs. How depressing! Just what did that Amish woman think she was doing by forcing her to read that book? She certainly hoped there wouldn't be a test on it.

Tiffany paced up and down the room for what seemed like an age, and then a thought occurred to her. What if she escaped? Her spirits soon plummeted. Where would she go? She couldn't go to her mother's as her mother would only drag her straight back to Eden. None of her friends were in town at the moment—not that she had any friends —and that only left Cameron. She couldn't even get in touch with him because her phone had been confiscated.

Tiffany sat back down on the bed and pulled the heavy book onto her knees. She had no choice. It was either die of utter boredom, or read this book.

CHAPTER 11

Tiffany

iffany was horrified to read of the true-life story of Dirk Willems. He was imprisoned in a tower for the crime of promoting re-baptism, adult baptism. He escaped by tying pieces of cloth together and then climbing down the walls. One guard chased him, but he made his escape over thin ice. However, the guard fell into the freezing water, and would have died, only Dirk came back and saved his life. For that, Dirk was recaptured, and later burned at the stake.

Tiffany stared at the illustration on the

yellowing pages. She was so engrossed that she didn't hear Miriam open her door. "Lunch is ready, Tiffany. Would you like to come down?" With that, Miriam left.

Tiffany shut the book and then looked at it. It wasn't as boring as she had first thought.

When Tiffany reached the kitchen, she was surprised to see another Amish woman sitting there, at the table. Tiffany guessed she was about her age.

Miriam did the introductions. "Tiffany, this is Martha. She used to be my assistant, but then she married James."

Tiffany nodded shyly to Martha. She was married already? Still, Tiffany knew several girls her own age who were married. "Hello," she said awkwardly.

"*Hiya*, Tiffany. Miriam tells me you're doing my old job." She shot at Tiffany what appeared to Tiffany to be a genuine smile.

Tiffany was surprised that Miriam didn't make a sarcastic remark, or say that she was no help at all. In fact, even Ethan remained silent, but smiled in response. She was beginning to see that these Amish truly were kindhearted and forgiving. She expected that every one of them would go and rescue a drowning guard from an icy pond, even if that man later burned them at stake. Tiffany would have just left the guard there to drown. She shifted in her seat, uncomfortable at admitting such a thing. Did that make her a bad person? Perhaps she really couldn't leave someone to drown. She looked up to see Martha looking at her.

"Are you enjoying the work so far?"

Tiffany narrowed her eyes, but it seemed as if Miriam had not in fact complained about her to the others. That surprised her. "It's hard work," she said. "It's much harder work than I thought."

Martha laughed. "You'll get used to it. It sure is hard work, but there's nothing quite so rewarding as coming to the end of a hard day's work and knowing you've given it your all, is there?"

Tiffany had quite the opposite point of view, but she was not about to say that out loud. Tiffany could not help but notice the way James and Martha exchanged loving glances. In fact, they could hardly take their eyes off each other. That was the kind of relationship she had always wanted.

"James was just telling me about all the excitement this morning," Martha continued. "Miriam, you don't really think those coins could be part of Captain Kidd's lost treasure, do you?"

Miriam shrugged. "Oscar Leadman couldn't

find any more, and the whole water trough is out of the ground now. He dug around in that hole for quite a long time and didn't find anything else. If it is treasure, then it's strange that there were only five coins. Perhaps they're recent coins."

"And the sheriff questioned all the guests and has no idea what happened to the coins," Jonas added.

"Were the coins valuable?" Tiffany asked, interested in spite of herself.

Jonas shrugged. "The sheriff didn't know. I was going to take them to show an expert in town, but they were stolen before I could."

"Have the reporters been back?" Martha asked. "It won't be good if anything else is stolen from Eden."

Miriam shook her head. "The reporters haven't actually come to the door again, but they've been driving backward and forward past the property."

"Who alerted them to the discovery?" Martha asked.

Miriam said she didn't know, and continued to discuss the treasure, the theft, and the journalists. For once, Tiffany wasn't the center of attention, and she liked it. This surprised her, because she usually *did* like to be the center of attention. To her surprise, she found it relaxing to be in a happy group of people where she was not getting into trouble for anything.

Suddenly, everything went quiet and the others shut their eyes. Tiffany wondered how long she would take to get used to this, the short silent prayer before every meal. They opened their eyes, and at once, Ethan passed her a plate of scalloped potatoes, along with beef and carrots. There was also a huge gravy boat, and plates of baked corn as well as salad.

Tiffany ate greedily. The work had made her ravenous. When Miriam left to fetch the desserts, Tiffany and Martha both followed to help. "What's that?" Tiffany asked, pointing to a large bowl that Miriam had just removed from the refrigerator.

"That's Dutch Cracker Pudding," Miriam said. "We're making some for dinner this evening, so I'll show you how to make it later. It's simple really, mainly eggs, cornstarch, butter, and brown sugar. Oh, and the crackers, of course." She handed Tiffany a bowl of peaches to take to the table. "The Dutch Cracker Pudding we're about to eat also has coconut in it."

Tiffany happened to look out the window at that moment, and could see Phyllis and Murray

Woods standing, looking at the place where the coins had been found. After a moment, Murray got down on his knees and seemed to be digging in the dirt with his hands. Miriam walked up and looked over her shoulder. "They must be interested in the treasure," she said calmly before walking back to the others.

Tiffany was a little suspicious of the couple. She knew she hadn't called the newspaper to tell them about the coins, so she wondered if Phyllis and Murray had. In her short time at Eden, she knew they didn't really relate to the other guests and tended to keep to themselves. Were they up to something? Tiffany was beginning to feel a little protective toward Eden. She'd have to keep an eye on the guests. That would make her stay less boring, at least.

Tiffany enjoyed the easy conversation over the Dutch Cracker Pudding and the fruit. The saltiness of the crackers contrasted beautifully with the sweetness of the coconut. When she said that to Miriam, Miriam told her that the Dutch Cracker Pudding they were making later would use graham crackers so wouldn't be as salty. Tiffany smiled to herself. Who would have thought she would enjoy having lunch with a group of Amish people? She looked up and caught Ethan's eye. He at once looked away, and his face turned beet red.

Tiffany was surprised. She had only seen men do that before when they were attracted to her. Surely an Amish man wouldn't be attracted to her? She thought Amish men were only attracted to Amish women, the type who would rescue prison guards from an icy pond only to suffer for their good deed later. She was not so noble. She knew she was spoiled, and she was given to tantrums, so what would an Amish man see in her?

And more to the point, why was she thinking this way? As handsome as Ethan was, she couldn't live the life of an Amish person. No TV, no internet, all the cooking and cleaning. Oh, and no driving cars. Actually, now that she thought about it, she hadn't missed her car. She did miss her phone and she missed being on social media. Still, she was grateful for the way the Amish had accepted her into their group. There was none of that underlying spitefulness and jealousy that she had noticed with the women who were supposed to be her friends.

Miriam watched Tiffany as she ate her lunch. She was enormously relieved that the young woman was settling in, to some degree. Tiffany seemed to be transforming before her very eyes, and she had actually been reading the *Martyrs Mirror* when she had called for her earlier. Yet while Miriam was relieved about that, she was disturbed to see the way Tiffany kept looking at Ethan. In fact, she couldn't seem to take her eyes off him. Ethan seemed to feel the same way.

Miriam shook her head. She couldn't see a young woman like Tiffany settling down into the Amish way of life. Surely she was too attached to her flashy clothes, her car, and the family's money. Miriam didn't want to see Ethan's feelings getting hurt. She decided she would have a word to Jonas later about the situation.

CHAPTER 12

Tiffany

———

or the next week, Tiffany settled into work at Eden, surprising herself. She was becoming used to the work there, and what's more, she was enjoying the easy companionship with Miriam, Jonas, James, and Ethan—especially Ethan.

She loved the sense of family. She loved the way they all chatted over dinner and each was genuinely interested in what the others had to say. Tiffany wasn't used to this type of experience. While she was sure her parents loved her in their on way, they had always been too busy for her. For as long as she could remember, her parents always ate while watching TV, and never sat around the table talking happily. In fact, it had been rare that her parents had spoken to her at all. They were always concerned with the business, and their financial affairs. She was an only child, so she had no siblings to play with or to confide in, and her friends only seemed more interested in themselves.

Tiffany had always thought she'd had a rich, privileged upbringing, but now that she was at Eden, she was beginning to see that they had riches in other ways.

She still couldn't get used to getting up at five in the morning, so she was grateful for the fact that Amish coffee was strong. This morning she was scrubbing the kitchen floors when Miriam came up to her and handed her some car keys. Tiffany had them in her hand before she realized they were keys to her own car.

"Would you be able to drive Ethan to town today please, Tiffany?" Tiffany stood there with her jaw open, so Miriam continued. "He needs a ride to town because my buggy has been in to be fixed, and

Mr. Fischer has let me leave my horse with him. Ethan needs to drive my buggy and my horse home. I'll give you a list of supplies to buy for me too, if that's all right."

Tiffany couldn't have been more excited. She had not left Eden for a week, and was thrilled about the thought of going back into town, especially with the handsome Ethan.

"Now, don't speak to any reporters if they see you," Miriam cautioned her.

Tiffany shook her head. "I haven't seen any around for a while."

"They call several times a day," Miriam said. "I thought they would've given up by now."

Tiffany went back to her work with renewed vigor. She was looking forward to taking Ethan to town. He seemed interested in her, but she couldn't trust her own judgment. What did she know about these things? She'd never had a boyfriend, unless you could count Cameron, and he wasn't a real boyfriend, just a man who seemed interested in her. His parents were friends with her parents.

It seemed like forever before Ethan came over and said it was time to go to town. "Just let me get the list that Miriam left for me," Tiffany said, wiping her hands on her apron. She walked as fast as she could to the kitchen, took off her apron, and collected her list. She wished she had time to put on make-up, but upon reflection, Ethan probably was repulsed by make-up, given that no Amish women wore it. Perhaps it was better that she had the natural look.

Tiffany smiled when the engine cranked over, but then frowned as the noise seemed so loud to her ears.

"Is something wrong?" Ethan asked her.

She looked at him, the way his muscles rippled under his shirt, his strong arms and strong hands. "It's funny, but I've been in Eden for over a week now, and it's so quiet here, so the engine gave me a little fright." She laughed nervously.

Ethan nodded. "Yes, that's to be expected," he said. "That's how I feel every time I go into town. I leave the tranquility and calm of my life and head into a rush. It's like a different time."

Tiffany smiled at him and he returned her smile. Her stomach twisted into one big knot. She drove off slowly, not at her usual speed. She saw some Amish buggies on the way, so she slowed down and then gave them a wide berth.

"They would appreciate that," Ethan said after

they passed the fifth one. "I don't think many drivers understand just how easily our horses are frightened. They see us on the roads all the time, so I'm sure they think horses are used to traffic, but that isn't always the case. Besides, some horses are young and nervous."

"I hadn't actually thought of that," Tiffany said. They were close to town now. "Tell me where Mr. Fischer's establishment is."

"He's on the edge of town," Ethan said, "but I do have to run a few errands first. Would it be too much of an imposition if you took me into town first and then I could do my errands, while you ran the errands for Mrs. Berkholder. After that, you could give me a ride back to Mr. Fischer's."

Tiffany was thrilled with the opportunity to be with Ethan longer, but she tried to fix her features into a careful lack of expression. "Sure. I don't mind at all." She silently berated herself for showing too much enthusiasm in her voice, but Ethan merely smiled at her.

"If you could take me to Tracking Street and leave me there, and then I can meet you back there." Tiffany was about to agree, when he continued. "There's a café on the corner of Tracking Street. Why don't we meet there later?

That way, if one of us is running late, the other one will at least be comfortable."

Tiffany agreed. She hoped that Ethan would ask her for coffee, but then again she didn't know if that was the Amish thing to do. Besides, surely he wouldn't have coffee with a woman who wasn't Amish. From what she knew about the Amish, asking someone on a buggy ride was their way of dating.

Tiffany was pleased to see the little grocery store that Miriam had told her about was quite close to Tracking Street. At first she felt self-conscious, not being in her high heels and make-up, but then she decided that she didn't really care. In a way, there was something nice and refreshing about being comfortable in one's own skin.

Tiffany did all the shopping, and then checked her list. When she was certain she had everything, she paid the cashier and then walked to her car. She looked at her watch. Truth be told, Tiffany had rushed to fulfill her duties as fast as she could so she could get to the little café early. She saw with relief that Ethan wasn't already waiting there. She figured she would order as fast as she could and then Ethan would have to wait for her to finish her coffee and cake. After all, it would be impolite for him to ask her to leave, and the Amish were never impolite.

Tiffany smiled at herself, pleased with her plan. After she ordered, she sat at a table with a good view over the street. There was no sign of Ethan, so she would eat her cake slowly. It was only after the waitress deposited her coffee and her cake in front of her, that she realized she had ordered a wet bottom shoo fly pie. Tiffany nearly laughed aloud. Perhaps she was in danger of becoming Amish, after all. She looked at the menu and saw giant apple fritters and whoopie pies, but then there were the non-Amish cookies and pastries as well.

Tiffany took a bite of the shoo fly pie and realized it was not as good as Miriam's. She would have to ask Miriam to show her how to make it. She enjoyed helping Miriam bake. In fact, she found it more fun than being on social media.

"Tiffany."

Tiffany looked up to see Ethan standing over her. She at once felt guilty for eating. What if he was in a hurry? She regretted her plan. To her relief, Ethan sat opposite her. "That shoo fly pie looks good."

"I was just thinking that it's not as good as Miriam's," Tiffany said with a laugh.

Ethan joined in her laughter. "Well, it looks as if you haven't started your coffee yet. Mind if I order some coffee and cake too?"

Tiffany hoped that her delight was not showing on her face. "Sure."

Soon the two of them were sitting there, over coffee and cake, chatting away like two old friends. Tiffany felt quite comfortable speaking to Ethan; it was if she had known him for years. All too soon they had both finished their coffee and cake, and so stood up to leave. If anyone in the café had thought it strange that an Amish man and a non-Amish woman were having coffee together, they gave no sign.

As the two of them walked along Tracking Street to Tiffany's car, they passed a non-descript looking store with a large sign in the window, *Buy and sell old jewelry and coins. Highest prices paid for scrap gold*.

Tiffany would not have taken too much notice, only she saw Delia Wilson inside. "Ethan," she said urgently, "that's Delia Wilson, one of the guests at Eden."

Ethan raised his eyebrows. "Why does that concern you?"

Tiffany at once felt foolish. "You know, the

treasure at Eden," she said. "Everyone said it was strange that only a few coins were found. Delia was looking around the area—I saw her myself. What if she stole some of the treasure and she's in there selling it right now?"

CHAPTER 13

Tiffany

*T*iffany was glad that Ethan didn't dismiss her statement as foolish. Instead, he seemed to be considering her words seriously. He stopped and looked through the window. "We could go in there, but it's a small store and she'll see us."

Tiffany bit her lip. "Let's go in there, anyway. We might find out something."

To her relief, Ethan agreed. The two of them walked into the store, but instead of acting nervous, Delia greeted them warmly. "Why, if it isn't Tiffany and Ethan. What are you two doing here?"

"Mrs. Berkholder asked me to give Ethan a ride to collect her buggy and we were just on our way to collect the buggy when we saw you in here," Tiffany said truthfully.

Delia smiled. Tiffany thought that perhaps she had judged her wrongly, given that she was certainly not acting furtively. "Frank was always interested in old coins," she said. "When I was married to that dreadful man, I wasn't interested in coins, but now that we're divorced, I have to admit that I *am* a little interested." She handed a coin to Tiffany. "This is one of the coins from the age of Captain Kidd."

Tiffany gasped. "Do you mean it's a pirate coin?"

The store owner nodded. "Yes, definitely. It's a colonial Spanish club coin, pirate money for sure. It's from the sixteenth century."

Tiffany's mouth fell open. "It must be worth a fortune!" She hurriedly handed it back to Delia.

The store owner laughed. "That one's worth thirteen dollars."

Tiffany wasn't sure if she had heard him correctly. "But I thought it would be worth a fortune!" she said.

The store owner laughed. "No. It depends on the condition, of course. That one's a copper and silver composition, not gold, and it's in rather bad condition. See, there's a large triangular chip out of it."

"How much would it be worth if it was gold?" Tiffany asked him.

The store owner shrugged. "About thirty dollars, I suppose."

"I always thought gold coins would be worth a lot more," Tiffany said.

"You can even buy ancient Roman and ancient Greek coins for quite a reasonable price," the store owner said. "Condition is everything. Of course, if they're gold, they can be melted down, and the gold price is quite high at the moment." He eyed Tiffany speculatively. "Do you have any gold jewelry you'd like to sell?"

Tiffany shook her head. She was thinking of the coins that were found at Eden. Why did the coins appear, and then disappear if they weren't worth much? Perhaps whoever stole them thought as she had, that gold coins were worth more. "Has anyone tried to sell you any old coins lately?" she asked him.

He shook his head. "Not in the last day or so, but people always sell me coins. That's how I get my stock, mostly from the public, of course."

Delia had lost interest in the conversation and was looking at coins again. Tiffany turned back to the store owner. "That coin I was just looking at—what would it be worth, if it was in gold and in that condition? I suppose I'm asking what it would be worth if it was melted down. Would gold coins be worth more melted down than in their original state?" She hoped what she said made sense, because it sounded rather garbled to her own ears.

"Like I said, it would depend on the condition, but a few coins like that wouldn't be worth a great deal."

"What do you mean?" Tiffany pressed him.

He shrugged. "Two, three hundred dollars. Not a fortune, if that's what you're thinking."

"Are you thinking of the coins stolen at Eden?" Delia asked her. "I thought they'd be worth a lot more than that, too. I would've guessed several thousand dollars at least. Well, isn't that interesting." She chewed a fingernail.

The store owner leaned across the counter. "Eden? The Bed and Breakfast where Captain Kidd's treasure is rumored to be?"

Tiffany muttered something and then shot a look at Ethan. They said their goodbyes to Delia and hurried out of the store. "What did you think of that?" Tiffany said excitedly. "Delia was one of my suspects. I saw her right where the old water trough had been dug up and she was acting furtively."

Ethan stroked his chin. "And did you see how disappointed she sounded when she found out that the coins weren't worth much?"

Tiffany nodded. "Yes, I did. Do you know, she might've even had the stolen coins in her purse right then and been about to sell them to the store owner."

Ethan frowned deeply. "Surely she wouldn't be so bold as to sell them in the same town. Surely she would wait until she went home to wherever she came from."

Tiffany was crestfallen. "Oh, silly me. Of course you're right."

"But you did an amazing job of questioning the store owner," Ethan said with clear admiration. "And perhaps Delia was in there finding out how much coins that age were worth. After all, she was looking at a seventeenth century pirate coin."

Tiffany's spirits at once lifted. "You're right!" Tiffany was pleased that Ethan had praised her. She had never been given much praise in her life. In fact, she couldn't remember the last time she had been praised. No matter how well she had done at school, her parents had always told her that she should have done better. Nothing was ever good enough for them. They always told her she had to strive harder and not be complacent. Even when she once won an essay competition, they told her that the other essays must have been particularly bad for hers to win.

"You really should be careful though, Tiffany," Ethan said. "We didn't know those coins weren't worth a fortune. Delia probably thought they were worth thousands as well, so whoever stole them might think the same thing and be back for more."

Butterflies fluttered through Tiffany's stomach when Ethan expressed concern for her safety. "It had to be one of the guests, you know," she said. "Simon Gibson, Delia, or Phyllis and Murray Woods. Those two always act suspiciously. I know they're hiding something."

"The thing that puzzles me," Ethan said, "is, who called the newspaper? You wouldn't think a thief would do that."

Tiffany let out a squeal as she stepped in a puddle beside her car. She had been so interested in the conversation and Ethan's company that she hadn't been watching where she was going. "Yes, that's a complete mystery," she said. "It doesn't make sense."

They discussed the matter of the stolen coins on the way to Mr. Fischer's, but came to no conclusions.

As Tiffany stopped the car, she looked with interest at the horses and buggies tied up in a line beside where she had just parked her car. "I've never been in a buggy before."

Ethan smiled at her. "I must take you for a buggy ride sometime." With that, he was gone.

Tiffany started her car and pulled back onto the road. She was halfway back to Eden before she realized what Ethan had said. To the Amish, a buggy ride meant a date. Her cheeks flushed hot. But is that what Ethan had meant?

CHAPTER 14

Tiffany

*M*iriam was grateful when Tiffany returned with the supplies. The two women chatted happily as they unpacked the groceries. When Jonas walked into the kitchen, Tiffany noticed the way Miriam's cheeks flushed beet red and her hands nervously folded into her apron.

"Have you asked Tiffany about the website yet?" he asked and then left with a wink.

"Website?" Tiffany said.

"Jonas suggested that Eden needs a website to

attract guests, now that the renovations are going nicely and we have more available rooms," Miriam explained.

"And Amish people aren't allowed to do websites?" Tiffany guessed.

Miriam laughed. "Actually, it depends on the bishop in each community. There is no one general rule for all Amish people, like some seem to think. In most communities, including ours, the Bishop allows businesses to use websites as well as electricity." Miriam laughed at the look on Tiffany's face. "I'm sure you've noticed electric lights when you go into any Amish store," she said.

It was Tiffany's turn to smile. "I've never thought about it like that," she said. "But the internet? Isn't that a bit too modern?"

Miriam shrugged. "We have to make a living in this day and age. We're not *of* the world, but we're *in* the world."

Tiffany was fascinated. The Amish certainly seemed to be a people of contradiction. And was Miriam really going to let her near a computer? And on the internet at that? "So you don't have a website at all?"

Miriam shook her head. "Jonas has been suggesting it for a while, and so has my daughter,

Rachel. We just didn't know anyone who could do it. Do you know someone?"

"I'll do it!" Tiffany said.

Miriam looked doubtful. "But isn't a website a very difficult thing to set up?"

Tiffany smiled. "I did computer science at school. I'll have you a wonderful website up and running in no time." Then something occurred to her. "Um, does your website need to be black and white? You know, kind of, um, plain?"

Miriam appeared to be confused by her question. "I'm not sure what you mean. I don't know anything about websites."

Tiffany wondered how to explain. "Do other people in the community have websites? You know, other Amish businesses? If you could tell me some names, then I can have a look at their websites and see what they're like. Then I could actually make you up a website. You could approve it and make suggestions before it went live." Seeing Miriam was looking more and more confused, Tiffany added, "I mean, I can make a website, but you and I will be the only ones who see it until you approve it."

Miriam's face lit up. "That would be wonderful. *Denki*, Tiffany. When can you start?"

"How about now? I do have my laptop with me.

I will need the internet password, though." She narrowed her eyes, wondering if Miriam would object and then wondering how she was going to explain that she wouldn't be able to build a website without the internet. To her relief, Miriam readily agreed.

"Where would you like to work?" Miriam asked her. "You would need to sit by a nice window with a view. When I'm doing my crafts, and my hand piecing for my quilts, I always like to sit in that room with the view over the fields." She gestured to another room. "And Tiffany, when I have some more time, would you teach me about the website?"

"Are you allowed to use computers?" Tiffany said in disbelief.

Miriam nodded. "Yes, for business. In the community I came from in Ohio, one of the women did the website for the family business. As I said, it depends on the Bishop. These days, most Bishops allow us to use computers for business."

Well, you learn something every day, Tiffany thought.

Tiffany couldn't wait to get her hands on her laptop, and when she logged in, she breathed a sigh of relief. Miriam had given her a handwritten list of Amish businesses in the community that had websites. But first, Tiffany was going to check her

Facebook page. She did so surreptitiously, first glancing around to make sure no one could see her. To her dismay, not one Facebook friend had asked where she was. She used to post several times a day, mostly forwarding from her Instagram account, but no one had noticed that she'd been missing. She checked her friends' timelines and was surprised that she wasn't interested in their conversations.

"Perhaps the Amish ways are wearing off on me," she said quietly to herself.

Tiffany shut down her Facebook page and then looked through the Amish websites. One was very plain, all dark blue and white with no photos, but one of the others was the opposite extreme. It had an extensive menu, and bright photos. That was quite a professional website, and Tiffany didn't think she could match it, but she did know that she would be able to do a rather effective and beautiful website for Eden.

Tiffany paused to look out over the fields. It was a beautiful, sunny day with not a cloud to be seen. Tiffany had never really stopped to enjoy nature before, but was aware that her pace of life was starting to slow down even after the short time she had been at Eden. She was beginning to appreciate the way the Amish enjoyed every moment. They lived in the moment, rather than for the future. They regarded friendships as treasures and were genuinely interested in each other. She still thought they were a little weird, but she was now enjoying their company. In fact, she wondered how she would go back to her own world with her plastic, insincere friends.

CHAPTER 15

Tiffany

---

*T*iffany was delighted that Miriam was thrilled with the website. Miriam couldn't stop staring at the website. Tiffany wasn't used to people not criticizing her. While she figured her parents wanted the best for her, they had always criticized her, but now Miriam, who was little more than a stranger, told her she was competent and hard-working.

Tiffany had explained to Miriam that it was only the start of the website, and she would need to take photographs of the actual property, inside and out, to put on the website. She had hesitated to tell Miriam that, in case Miriam thought it was a ploy to ask for her phone back, so she was careful to add that she could take the photographs with her phone the following day.

And so, that afternoon, Tiffany found herself in the kitchen. She had offered to make apple dumplings for dinner that night. Truth be told, she wanted to impress Ethan. Jonas and Ethan stayed back for dinner most nights, while James went home to his wife, Martha. Sometimes Jonas and Ethan stayed after dinner for coffee, which they and the two women shared with the Eden guests.

The guests always went out for dinner and then came back to Eden, and seemed to enjoy sitting around talking about their day's activities over coffee. Yet Tiffany was certain that one of the guests was the thief. Maybe even more than one guest. But who? That was the question that had been keeping her awake at night.

Tiffany had never baked a thing in her life. Her parents had a chef to do that sort of thing, but she had been watching Miriam since she arrived at Eden. Looking at the recipe, she realized that observing was not enough.

What's more, she could barely read Miriam's

writing. Miriam had written out the recipe in a hurry, telling her that she had no written recipes. All Miriam's recipes were passed down from one generation to the other. "They're all in here," Miriam had said, tapping her head.

Tiffany put two cups of all-purpose flour in a bowl, along with two and a half teaspoons of baking powder, and a large pinch of salt. So far so good. Next she had to mix in the butter. Miriam often churned her own butter, from the milk provided by a neighbor's cow, but only when she had time. Tiffany had been fascinated by the bright yellow butter, a much deeper color than store-bought butter.

Tiffany wondered how she was expected to soften the butter. Perhaps she should have prepared it beforehand. She stabbed it with a knife until it was in small pieces and then wondered what to do next. She didn't think she had time to set it in the sun, so she filled a bowl of warm water, put the butter in the bowl and set the bowl in the hot water. That didn't work either, because the butter began to melt and the recipe hadn't mentioned melted butter. Tiffany didn't know anything about chemistry, but she still thought that might not be the best idea.

Tiffany finally got a wooden spoon, squashed

the butter and then stirred it. After what seemed an age, the butter seemed to be soft enough. Tiffany sighed with relief and wiped her forehead. She poured the butter into the bowl and then stirred it. It was lumpy. Tiffany shook her head in disgust. Who would have thought baking could be this difficult? Miriam had told her to stick to the recipe, and the recipe said to add half a cup of milk. Tiffany was stirring the mixture as vigorously as she could when Ethan came inside.

"What are you doing here?" she blurted out, only too aware that she was covered in flour, and then instantly regretted her words.

Ethan frowned, so she continued, "I'm just stressed, that's all. I'm making apple dumplings and I've never baked before."

Ethan was pouring himself a glass of water, and he looked up in shock. "What? You've never done any baking before? *Sell kann ennichpepper duh!*"

Tiffany looked up from her stirring. "What does that mean?"

The young man's cheeks flushed. "I'm so sorry. It just means that anyone can do it."

He looked so embarrassed for his words, that Tiffany hurried to reassure him. "Yes, it's just that I've never learned."

"What are you making?" Ethan asked her.

"Apple dumplings," Tiffany said with a tremor in her voice. "I'm trying to make the dough now. Then I have to divide it into balls and roll out each ball."

Ethan pointed to the dough. "Be gentle with the dough. It will come out hard if you're so rough with it."

"Thanks." Tiffany bit her lip. "I thought Amish men didn't know anything about baking?"

Ethan shrugged. "I don't have any brothers, only sisters. Besides, all Amish men have to know some things about baking. What if their wives are sick? Or are expecting?"

Tiffany was embarrassed to feel a slow red flush crawl up her face. What was wrong with her? He had only said 'expecting,' and that was hardly something to make her blush. She didn't blush when her friends swore, so why was she blushing now? "Thanks, I'll try to do it like that. I don't suppose you could show me how?"

Ethan looked worried. He looked around the room, and then hurried over. "I haven't washed my hands," he said hopefully.

"Well, there's no time like the present." Tiffany nodded to a bar of soap on the countertop.

Ethan sighed with resignation. He washed his hands and then returned moments later. "You just have to knead it gently like this," he said. "You don't want to knock all the air out of it. Now you try."

Tiffany always hated doing things in front of other people, because she had always been criticized in the past, but she had no choice. She tried to copy what Ethan did, and then looked up at him.

"*Wunderbaar!*"

Tiffany did not know what the word meant, but given the way Ethan was smiling and clasping his hands together, she figured it was good. "Did I do it right?"

Ethan nodded. "Yes, you did. You'll be baking in no time. Just one more tip for you, before you pour the applesauce over the dumplings, make holes in the dough first."

Tiffany was going to reply, but Jonas and James walked into the kitchen at that moment, along with Miriam. Ethan scurried out as fast as he could. Tiffany noticed that Miriam and Jonas exchanged glances. "How is your baking coming along, Tiffany?" Miriam asked her.

"Ethan just showed me how to knead pastry,"

Tiffany said. "I just have to roll the balls out now and then I have to make the apple mixture."

Miriam nodded. "It all looks like it's coming along nicely. You're doing well for your first attempt. Jonas and I are just going onto the front porch to see how the work's progressing, so if you need help, you'll find us there."

When they were on the front porch, Miriam turned to Jonas. "Are you worried about that?"

Jonas chuckled. "Do you mean Tiffany's crush on Ethan, or Ethan's crush on Tiffany?"

"Jonas, I'm not sure it's a laughing matter." Miriam folded her arms and frowned. "She's an *Englischer* and from a life of privilege."

Jonas kept smiling. "*Es gebt viele schwatze kieh, awwer sie gewwe all weissi millich,*" he said with a twinkle in his eye.

"Sorry?"

"It means there are many black cows, but all give white milk."

Miriam put her hands on her hips. "I know full well what it means, Jonas," she said. "I just don't see what relevance that proverb has to this situation."

"The Bible says we're all the same; there's neither Jew nor Greek, rich or poor. God sees us all as the same."

"Yes, that is true, but *Englischers* don't usually marry Amish."

Jonas was still smiling. "*Gott* works in mysterious ways."

Miriam finally laughed. "Jonas, I'll be calling you *Scripture Smart* in a moment. Well then, if you're not worried, I'll try not to be worried. I just don't want to see either one of them get hurt."

Jonas turned his attention to the barrier around the end of the porch. "Nor do I, but they're grown people and not our children."

A little thrill of excitement ran through Miriam when he said *our children*. Jonas seemed to have realized what he said, because he paused for a moment, before continuing his work.

Miriam had been in love with Jonas for quite some time now and she was fairly confident that he returned her feelings. There was a kind of ease, of comfort between them as well as more than a spark of attraction. So why didn't Jonas want to date her? Her own husband had gone to be with *Gott*, and

Jonas's *fraa* had gone to be with *Gott* even earlier than that. Was it possible that Jonas was still pining for his lost *fraa*? What other reason could there be?

Miriam thoughts turned to Tiffany as she watched Jonas work. It was clear to her that there was an attraction between Tiffany and Ethan, and while Tiffany had turned from a spoiled princess to a nicer person in a short space of time, she was hardly an Amish woman. Was there any future for Tiffany and Ethan?

CHAPTER 16

Tiffany

*T*iffany had been unable to sleep. She tossed and turned, thinking of Ethan. She had been asked on many dates, but had always refused. She wanted the kind of love that would make her heart leap, the kind of love where she could grow old with someone. Forever love.

Was she falling in love with Ethan? She thought so. She had never been in love before, but she wasn't worried about that. She had always wanted to be in love with just one man.

Tiffany tossed and turned, but still couldn't

sleep. She wasn't always a good sleeper, but in the past, she would have watched a YouTube video. Of course, that was out of the question here.

Tiffany finally gave up trying to sleep and sat on the edge of her bed. What she really wanted was some hot chocolate, but was she brave enough to leave her room when the thief might be out there? Tiffany sat there weighing up her options. No one had been harmed and that hot chocolate was calling to her. Besides, it wasn't as if she was alone in the house. All she had to do was scream, and several people would come running.

With that in mind, Tiffany threw on some clothes and then gingerly opened her door. She crept along the corridor, her heart in her mouth. No amount of self talk could prepare her for walking along a dark corridor in the middle of the night.

The moon had shone brightly into her bedroom, but here, along the dark corridors, she could barely see in front of her nose. And, of course, she was not going to turn on the lights and alert everyone to her presence.

When Tiffany reached the bottom of the stairs, she froze in horror. Someone was ahead of her right at the front door. She clutched the wall for support and held her breath. This must be the culprit! Tiffany wanted nothing more than to turn and run back to her room, but curiosity got the better of her. She crept along, following the figure.

The front door closed, so Tiffany skirted around to look out the window. She would be able to get a good view from there. Tiffany was relieved that she only saw one person.

Tiffany peeked around the edge of the curtain and then jumped back in shock. She expected to see whoever it was continuing down to the fields, but this person was standing on the porch. She took a deep breath and then pulled the curtain back a little.

Just then, a cloud moved away from the moon and the person was bathed in moonlight. It was Simon Gibson! But what was he doing? Tiffany opened the curtain a little further. She couldn't quite see what he was doing, but he was bending down at the edge of the porch, right where Ethan, James, and Jonas had been working earlier.

Perhaps he only wanted some night air. Perhaps he, too, had been unable to sleep. Tiffany watched until Simon straightened back up and turned toward the door. She hurried to the kitchen and then turned on the light.

Tiffany figured that if Simon had been unable to sleep, then he would see the kitchen light and would come over, perhaps even to make himself some hot chocolate, or simply to speak. That, surely, is what an innocent person would do.

Yet Simon didn't come. Tiffany was even careful to make a little noise in the kitchen so that he would know someone was there. She sat and drank her hot chocolate at the kitchen table, feeling braver now. She figured she couldn't be in danger from Simon even if he was acting suspiciously. There was nothing outside to steal so perhaps he wasn't the thief.

Tiffany rinsed her cup and then went back to bed. She would tell Miriam about Simon's nighttime wanderings in the morning.

CHAPTER 17

Miriam

*W*hen Miriam went down to the kitchen to make *kaffi* the next morning, she was shocked beyond measure to see the coffee pot already simmering away, and Tiffany standing over it. "Tiffany!" she shrieked, before she could stop herself.

Tiffany swung around, a smile on her face. "I thought I'd get up early, with so much work to be done today. I wasn't able to sleep last night and I wanted to tell you what happened." Before Miriam could say anything, she pressed on. "I couldn't sleep, so I came downstairs to get some hot chocolate, but Simon Gibson was creeping along ahead of me. He went outside so I peeked through the window to see where he was going and he was crouching down at the end of the porch, where the men had been working."

Miriam frowned. "Did you see what he was doing?"

"No, unfortunately. I really want to figure out what happened to the stolen coins."

Miriam shook her head. "*Nee*, Tiffany, leave it be. Asking questions could be dangerous."

Tiffany smiled. "I'm not going to ask anyone any questions; I'm just going to think about it." She stared off into the distance.

At that moment, Miriam was struck by a realization. Had Tiffany gotten up early simply to speak to her in private about something, something other than seeing Simon walking about at night? She could hardly come out and ask, so she sat down at the kitchen table. "*Denki* for making coffee, Tiffany."

Tiffany poured coffee for both of them and then sat opposite Miriam. She twirled her cup around a few times, while Miriam sat patiently.

Finally, Tiffany spoke. "There's a man called

Cameron who keeps asking me on a date, but I haven't said yes." She looked at Miriam, so Miriam nodded in encouragement. Tiffany continued. "My parents say he doesn't like me for me, but he only likes me for my money." She paused again, but this time did not continue speaking.

"And what is your opinion on the matter?" Miriam asked her.

Tiffany shrugged. "I have no idea how someone knows when a man likes them for themselves. I'd like to feel a certainty that someone does like me. I'd like to have someone in my life who I don't doubt, someone I *know* is the right person. How do I know when I find that person?"

Miriam wondered if she was referring to Ethan, or to Cameron. "Do you think Cameron is the right man for you?"

Tiffany shuddered. "No way!" She pulled a face. "What do you think of true love? Do you think it's a fairytale? Or do you think it's possible?"

Miriam thought before speaking. "I know that various people have different opinions on this, but this is what I know. We believe that *Gott* has a special man and a special woman chosen for each other, that they are predestined."

Tiffany's eyebrows shot up. "As in soul mates? One true love, like in Disney movies?"

Miriam smiled. "I haven't seen a Disney movie, but we do believe that *Gott* has selected a husband and a wife for each other."

Tiffany appeared to be pondering her words. Miriam sipped her *kaffi* while waiting for Tiffany to speak again.

"Is that only Amish people?" Tiffany said.

Miriam was somewhat confused. "Is what only Amish people?"

Tiffany sipped her coffee before answering. "Has God only selected a husband and wife for Amish people, but not for others?"

Miriam poured herself another coffee. "I don't believe so. Why would God have one set of rules for one of His people and not for others?" She returned to her seat and looked Tiffany. The young woman was deep in thought.

"Do Amish men only marry Amish women?" Tiffany finally said, avoiding Miriam's gaze.

So that's what this is all about, Miriam thought. Aloud she said, "An Amish man can only marry a woman who is already in the community. On the other hand, an Amish man could date an *Englischer* woman who had joined the community, and then marry her." She looked at Tiffany as she said that, and it seemed to her that Tiffany looked relieved. Miriam pressed on. "As you've seen for yourself, our ways are quite different. While we do use electricity and internet here at Eden for business, Amish people don't have either in their homes. And while phones are used for business, we don't have phones in our homes. Also, we live by a set of rules and regulations. Outsiders think us severe, perhaps, or at least unusual."

Tiffany tapped her chin. "So you don't drive cars, or have technology, so you don't have social media. But instead of contacting friends on Facebook, you have friends in real life."

Miriam smiled. "I'm not sure what you mean, but yes, we do have friends in real life," she said with a smile.

"Can you tell me more about the Amish?"

Miriam frowned. "Well, our clothes are handmade. Married men must grow beards. You've noticed James has a new beard; that's because he's newly married. Men are not permitted to grow mustaches. We women can't cut our hair, and we can't wear jewelry or patterned clothes. Eden is a business, so there's more technology, so don't expect the same in an Amish house. Amish homes use wringer washers for laundry. It's a lot of hard work."

Tiffany nodded. "Since Amish people don't watch TV at night, what do they do?"

"All sorts of things. They might read books, play games such as Scrabble, or talk to each other. Many people have hobbies."

Tiffany was clearly intrigued. "What sort of hobbies?"

"Gardening, horseback riding, fishing, riding bikes, or woodwork, perhaps." Miriam took a deep breath. "To return to your original question, if an *Englischer* wanted to marry an Amish person, then that *Englischer* would need to speak to the Bishop and then join the community. They would need to be in the community for some time before the Bishop would give them permission to marry. Someone should want to join the Amish due to our beliefs and way of life, not to find a marriage partner. But yes, it does happen, and if the person's heart is in the right place, then it shouldn't be too difficult."

Miriam wanted to ask Tiffany if she was considering becoming Amish, but she didn't want to put the girl on the spot.

It seemed strange to Miriam that Tiffany would

want to do so, but then again, she had known it to happen. An *Englischer* woman had entered her community back in Ohio, but that was years ago. She had noticed that Tiffany had given to not wearing any make-up, and she was working hard, and these changes had happened in a short space of time, but that was a far cry from joining the community. Still, she suspected Tiffany didn't have a very good home life and Tiffany had continually remarked on the sense of family she had found at Eden.

Just then, Miriam jumped to her feet and motioned for Tiffany to be quiet. "There's someone sneaking through the house!" she whispered.

CHAPTER 18

Tiffany

iffany's heart beat so loud that she was sure the intruder would hear her even from that distance. She followed Miriam, and the two women crept through the house.

They both rounded a corner only to see Phyllis and Murray Woods in front of them. The two were sneaking along, making every effort to be quiet. To Tiffany's horror, Phyllis turned around and saw them. She and Miriam clutched each other.

Phyllis tapped Murray's arm. Tiffany stood, frozen to the spot, as Phyllis and Murray approached them. Murray loomed over them. Finally, he spoke. "Sorry. We didn't mean to disturb anyone."

"What are you doing?" Miriam asked them.

Tiffany wondered what she could do. Jonas, James and Ethan didn't arrive this early. She could hardly run for help. Isaac and Rachel's house was the closest, and it would take ages to run there. She had given her car keys back to Miriam, and had no idea where they were.

"I do hope we didn't wake you up," Phyllis said.

Miriam shook her head. "No, we always start at five. What are you doing up so early?"

Phyllis and Murray exchanged glances. "Go on, Murray. You might as well tell them," Phyllis said. "It won't matter—they won't tell anyone."

Tiffany huddled closer to Miriam. What did Phyllis mean by not telling anyone? Surely they didn't mean to harm them? With tears forming in her eyes, she bit her lip. Was this the end? Was she going to die before having a family? She sent up a silent prayer to God to spare them.

"We have an appointment early in town and we just wanted to get an early start because we're so nervous," Phyllis said, completely confusing Tiffany. Maybe they didn't intend to kill them, after all.

"It's our son," Murray said. "Phyllis and I knew each other as teenagers, and when we were very young…" His voice broke off and Phyllis patted him reassuringly on the arm. "When we were very young," he started again, "we had a baby, and Phyllis's parents forced her to have him adopted out as soon as he was born. We weren't married; we were too young for that."

Phyllis dabbed at her eyes. "And my parents moved away, and Murray and I weren't allowed to see each other any more. In fact, we didn't see each other for years. I had no idea where he was or even if he was married, but then, five years ago, we had a chance meeting."

Murray put his arm around Phyllis and pulled her close. "Yes, and then we were married five months later. We've been searching for our son ever since, and we found him. What's more, he wants to speak to us, and we're meeting him today."

"Why, that's *wunderbaar*," Miriam said.

"It sure is!" Tiffany said more loudly than she intended. Her enthusiasm was heightened by the realization that Phyllis and Murray were simply loving parents rather than thieves or murderers. That explained why the two of them had been acting strangely. They had simply been nervous and filled with anticipation at seeing their son for the first time.

Yet this only left two suspects, Simon and Delia. Surely one of them had to be the thief. As soon as Phyllis and Murray left, Tiffany whispered that fact to Miriam.

"It seems so," she said, "and now we know why Murray and Phyllis seemed so nervous all the time. Simon's here for a few more days and Delia is here for another week."

Tiffany looked at her. She knew what Miriam wasn't saying. Was something else about to happen at Eden?

CHAPTER 19

Tiffany

iffany had spent the first part of the morning ironing sheets with a gas iron. She had protested that Eden had electricity, but Miriam had simply said that she was getting her accustomed to the Amish way of life.

Had Miriam guessed that she was falling in love with Ethan? Perhaps she had. At any rate, the gas iron seemed just as efficient as an electric one, not that Tiffany had ever done any ironing before.

Tiffany wondered what it would be like to be an Amish wife. While she was not too fond of most adults, she absolutely loved children. She wanted to have several of her own. The thought of having children with Ethan set her heart into a flutter. But how did he feel about her? And even if he did have feelings for her, she wasn't Amish. Still, she had gotten into the habit of praying every night, telling God all her problems and innermost thoughts. If what Miriam had said was true, and God had chosen a husband for her, then she would have to trust in Him. If He had chosen Ethan for her, then He would make a way for them to be together.

Tiffany had just finished the ironing and had folded the sheets nicely, just the way Miriam had shown her how to fold them. This housework thing wasn't as bad as she had initially thought. In fact, she enjoyed it.

She was going in search of Miriam to find out her next duties, when Jonas hurried into the house, followed by Ethan and James. Tiffany's heart leaped as it always did when she saw Ethan. "Where's Miriam?" Jonas said, but before Tiffany had a chance to answer, Miriam walked into the room.

"What's wrong?" she said.

Jonas held out his hands. "We found these gold coins just then."

Tiffany and Miriam hurried over to look at the

coins. The coins were gold and shiny, albeit dirty. "Where did you find them?" Miriam said breathlessly.

"Just out there under the porch," Jonas said. "We pulled up some more boards and they were right there."

"It's Simon Gibson!" Tiffany said. "I was telling Miriam about it earlier. I couldn't sleep so in the middle of the night I was on my way to the kitchen to make some hot chocolate when I saw Simon sneaking out of the house. I looked out the window and saw him crouch down at the end of the porch directly under one of the brass wall sconces."

"That's exactly where we found the coins!" Jonas said. "Why would he put coins there?"

At that very moment, Simon Gibson came down the stairs. "What's going on, guys?" he said.

Tiffany wasted no time in coming to the point. "Jonas found more gold coins."

Simon did his best to look surprised, or so it seemed to Tiffany.

"I saw you last night," Tiffany said. "Why did you put the coins under the porch?"

Simon stopped walking down the stairs and clutched at his stomach. "What did you say?"

Tiffany folded her arms over her chest. "I saw

you last night. I couldn't sleep, so I went to the kitchen to get to make a hot drink, but I saw you go outside and put something under the porch."

"You must be mistaken," Simon said. Tiffany noted that his voice was uneasy.

"I think it's time I called the sheriff," Jonas said. "Let's see what sense he can make of the situation."

Simon held up a hand. "Please don't! Please don't call the sheriff. I'll explain everything."

"Was it you who stole the coins?" Miriam asked him.

Simon hurried over to the group. "I didn't steal the coins; they were mine in the first place. When I saw a man partially dig out the trough one afternoon, I threw some of the coins in there that night."

"Why would you do such a thing?" Tiffany asked him.

Simon's face turned a pale shade of green. "I'm sorry to cause all this trouble, really I am. It was true what I told you, that I was sacked from my job. It's hard being a freelance journalist. To make a living, I really need to work full-time. An editor back home said he'd give me a job if I gave him a big story."

Tiffany was beginning to put two and two

together. "So you put the gold coins there so everyone would think that Capt Kidd's treasure had been found? And you were the one who called the reporters?" Simon nodded. "But why did you steal your own coins?"

"I didn't want any other reporters to get the scoop on the story, so I took those coins and I put them back with more coins under the porch. I was trying to make it look like a genuine find."

"But what would've happened when the experts said it wasn't Captain Kidd's treasure?" Jonas said.

Simon shrugged. "How would they prove it wasn't? They were genuine seventeenth century pirate coins that I put there. No one would be able to prove it either way. I've already written a rather good story about the treasure, and that's why I came down the stairs now. I was waiting until you found the treasure and then I was going to ask you not to give the story to anyone else."

"There will be no story," Miriam said firmly.

Simon made to protest, but Miriam continued. "If there *is* a story, then I will have to call the sheriff and tell him everything you've done."

Some color was beginning to return to Simon's cheeks. "But I haven't done anything illegal."

"Maybe not," Tiffany said, "but I don't think

your new editor would be happy to know that you had faked all of this just to get a job."

Simon looked upset, so upset that Tiffany felt sorry for him. "That was my last hope of getting a job," he said.

Tiffany had a brainwave. "Would a really good human interest story get you the job?"

Simon looked thoughtful. "Yes, if it was interesting enough. What is it?"

Tiffany smiled at him. "It's not my story to tell, but let me ask some people and I'll let you know later today." She was thinking of Phyllis and Murray's story.

Later, Tiffany and Miriam were having lunch with Jonas, Ethan, and James, enjoying apple dumplings with milk and sugar.

"*Denki*, Tiffany," Miriam said.

Tiffany was confused. "For what?"

"For solving the mystery and forgiving Simon for causing all the trouble."

Tiffany muttered something and smiled nervously as everyone's eyes were upon her, Ethan's particularly so. "Sell kann ennichpepper duh." *Anyone could do that.*

They all chuckled. "You've picked up some words, I see," Jonas said with a smile.

Miriam patted Tiffany's hand. "Yes, and she was even ironing with a gas iron this morning. We'll have her Amish in no time."

Jonas, James, and Miriam laughed loudly, but Ethan wasn't laughing. He shot Tiffany a strange look. If only she could know what was going on behind his eyes, those eyes the color of forget-me-not flowers.

CHAPTER 20

Tiffany

"*T*hanks for coming with me to see the Bishop," Tiffany said to Miriam, as Miriam drove the buggy back to Eden.

"*Gern ghesche*," Miriam said. "That means, *you're welcome*."

Tiffany sighed. "There's so much to learn. Do you think I'll ever be able to learn to drive a buggy?"

"You'll have to learn sooner or later, if you're going to be Amish," Miriam said with a chuckle.

"When we turn onto the quieter road, I'll give you the reins."

Tiffany gasped. "What if the horse bolts?"

Miriam seemed to find the remark particularly funny. "She's a quiet mare, but if anything happens, I'll simply take the reins back."

"The Bishop wasn't anywhere near as scary as I thought he would be," Tiffany admitted. "It's just that I was really intimidated when he kept asking me about my willingness to renounce the ways of the modern world and all that. Then he gave me the third degree about the strength of my faith. And what did he mean about my motives being pure?" Tiffany went on and on until she saw Miriam frowning. "Sorry to keep talking so much. It's just that it's such a big thing."

"It *is* a big thing," Miriam said. "You don't yet have any idea of what life in Amish community is really like. When we get back to Eden, how about you move into the little cabin behind the *haus*? Martha used to live in it when she was working for me, before she married James."

Tiffany gasped with delight. "Really? That would be wonderful."

"*Wunderbaar*," Miriam said. "You need to learn

Pennsylvania Dutch. You've already picked up some words from us, and it won't be as hard as you might think. I'll just speak in less English and more Pennsylvania Dutch to you from now on."

"To be honest, I'm a little stressed about the whole thing, but I'm sure it's the right thing to do," Tiffany said.

"You mentioned to the Bishop that your driving motivation for joining the Amish was the sense of *familye*?" Miriam said, guiding her horse over to the side of the road as a loud car roared past.

"Yes. Like I said, I'm an only child, and my parents never had time for me. They used to send me to my grandmother's in England for weeks every year. I always felt I was a nuisance to them, that they didn't want me under their feet. I've never had any close friends, and I've always liked animals more than people. I've just never felt I belonged anywhere." Tiffany's voice broke, and she composed herself before speaking again. "Miriam, you're more family to me than anyone else I've ever known."

Miriam leaned across and patted her hand. "It's good to know you didn't want to join the Amish because of Ethan."

Tiffany thought for a while before speaking. "I don't even know if Ethan likes me, but it was, um, having a crush on Ethan that made me think about being Amish." She could feel her cheeks burning as she said it and shot a glance at Miriam. Miriam didn't seem to mind, so she continued. "If Ethan doesn't like me and marries someone else, then I'll still want to be Amish. I want to *belong*. It's the sense of community that I realize I've been craving. At first I hated the hard work, but then I enjoyed it. This might sound crazy, but I've discovered that I like scrubbing something until it's clean. It's rewarding."

Miriam laughed. "It doesn't sound crazy at all."

"I really enjoy baking," Tiffany said. "And I like the way everyone has your back if you're Amish. Plus I've never liked the hustle and bustle of the city world. I've never told you this, but when I was a child, I used to play with a little Amish boy down by the river near my parents' B&B. His father even made me a little wooden boat. Perhaps I was meant to be Amish right from that time."

Miriam nodded. "*Gott* has a plan for everyone."

Tiffany would have dearly liked to ask Miriam about Jonas, but she knew it was not her place. She could see the way the two of them looked at each other, and as both their partners had passed away many years ago, she wondered why they weren't together now.

"How will your parents react to the news that you're joining the community?" Miriam asked her.

Tiffany shuddered and crossed her arms over her chest. "I don't think they'll take the news well. In fact, I think they'll be quite angry."

"When will you tell them?"

Tiffany thought for a moment. "You know, I should take my car back to them and give it back to them as soon as we get back to Eden. Then I'll catch a taxi back to Eden. Would that be all right?"

Miriam nodded. "Yes, of course. And I'm so relieved that you're going to continue to work for me from now on. I really need an assistant, although one who won't get married too soon and leave me."

Tiffany chuckled. "I think you're quite safe. The Bishop said I have to prove myself in the Amish community for a long time before he'll allow me to marry."

Just then, they came upon the quiet road, and the horse was trotting along slowly and steadily.

Miriam showed Tiffany how to hold the reins. "Yes, that's right. You're doing well. The thing to remember is that you have to be very gentle and don't make any sudden moves because that will hurt the horse's mouth. You must be very gentle and sensitive to what the horse is doing."

Tiffany was quite scared at first, but then soon got into the rhythm. "I can't believe I'm doing this!" she exclaimed. "This is fun." She shot a worried look at Miriam. "Are Amish allowed to have fun?" she said worriedly.

Miriam burst into laughter.

Miriam was worried about Tiffany. She had been gone for quite some time now. Had her mother convinced her not to join the community? Miriam imagined that Debra Bedshill wouldn't be thrilled with the news that her daughter was becoming Amish.

It was with great relief that Miriam saw a taxi pull up out the front of Eden. She hurried down the steps to greet a tearful Tiffany. "What happened?"

It was clear to Miriam that Tiffany was doing her best not to cry. "It was awful, much worse than I thought," Tiffany said between sobs. "She was very angry with me and said she disowned me."

"It would have been an awful shock for her," Miriam said in a placating tone. "I'm sure she'll get used to it, but it might take some time."

Tiffany simply nodded and wiped her eyes.

"Why don't you go and get washed up and then we'll both have some meadow tea. Would you like me to find you some Amish clothes? I still have some of Rachel's here that would fit you."

Tiffany's face brightened up. "You mean I can start today?"

Miriam could not resist chuckling. "Sure you can." Miriam could see a car coming quickly in the distance and she was pretty sure she knew who it was. "You run along, Tiffany, and I'll see you in the kitchen soon."

The fancy car slid to a stop and a red-faced Debra Bedshill jumped out. "How dare you convince my daughter to join your cult!" she screamed.

Miriam didn't know what to say so she just stood there with her mouth open in shock. "Good afternoon, Mrs. Bedshill," she said finally said politely.

"Don't you *Good afternoon Mrs. Bedshill* me!" the woman yelled at her. "I'm going to pay a lot of money for a cult buster to come and convince Tiffany that she's been brainwashed."

Miriam was at a loss for words. "You said your daughter was unruly and uncontrollable, and now she is polite. Isn't that a good thing?"

Debra's face grew even redder. "You're twisting my words. Of course she's subdued now, because she's joined your cult. I demand you hand her over to me now!"

"I'm not keeping her a prisoner," Miriam said patiently. "She is free to come or go as she chooses."

"She's not free at all, you silly woman!" Debra yelled. "It's a cult! She doesn't know what she's doing! And I'm not paying you a cent." With that, she got in her car, slammed the door so hard Miriam was surprised it didn't fall off, and drove away at great speed.

Miriam turned around to see Jonas, James, and Ethan standing behind her. "Are you all right, Miriam?" Jonas said, his eyes full of concern.

Miriam nodded. "*Jah, denki*. Debra Bedshill has never been the easiest person to deal with."

Jonas nodded. Miriam shot a glance at Ethan, figuring that this was the first he had heard that Tiffany was joining the Amish. His brows were knitted tightly together, and his normally tanned face was white.

CHAPTER 21

Tiffany

$\mathcal{T}$iffany went down to the river. She kneeled against the riverbed, running her hands through the rushing water. The current was strong, the water cool against her hot fingers. Every part of her felt flushed with the big changes happening in her life.

It was a relief to sit near the river now and watch its surface twinkling in the sunlight. The wind gently wafted through the grass. Tiffany heard the distant sounds of men working in the fields, and felt such a divine peace that she almost drifted away on the clouds of her imagination. She was so caught up in her dreams that she almost missed the sound of boots against the grass.

"Tiffany?"

She looked up to see Ethan, and something about him reminded her of her childhood. It was only after a minute she realized he was holding a hand-carved wooden boat, just like the one she had as a little girl, the one her mother threw away.

"I wanted to give you this."

Tiffany rose to her feet and accepted the boat, turning it over in her hands. "But why?"

It took her a moment to realize he was not just Ethan; he was *the* Ethan, *her* Ethan, the Ethan of her childhood. How could she have not known this earlier? Had they not spent afternoon after afternoon playing by a river just like this one, racing their boats in the gentle current?

"Because your mother threw your boat out. Don't you remember?"

"Of course I remember! I was devastated. I cried myself to sleep for five whole nights. But Ethan, is it really you?"

Ethan smiled, and Tiffany's heart raced even faster.

She placed the boat in the water and they

watched it float down the river, walking after it until Ethan scooped down to pick it up.

Tiffany smiled. "I wouldn't want another boat to be lost."

"That's all right," he said. "I can always make you another one."

"You made that boat?"

"Of course. My father showed me."

Tiffany had no time to reply. He reached out and took her hand.

All at once, Tiffany could imagine their future together. She thought of Ethan making boats for their children. She could see the two of them sitting by this very river and watching their children laugh and play..

Tiffany chided herself for not recognizing him sooner. How silly she had been. "I can't believe it's really you," she said in a small voice.

"I knew it was you the first moment I saw you again."

"But you never said."

"I didn't want to be inappropriate."

"Oh, Ethan." Tiffany squeezed his hand. "You can make boats?"

"Yes." He smiled again. "Tiffany?"

She looked into his forget-me-not blue eyes.

"I hope that in a year or two, I will have someone new to make a boat for."

"Ethan," Tiffany said, as her cheeks flushed with the promise of a thousand beautiful tomorrows, "I hope so, too."

Amish Romance

Miriam is doing her best to cope with an influx of guests, when the sheriff calls by to warn her that a cat burglar has struck in the area. Could the thief be numbered amongst her guests? Miriam begins seeing her guests in a new light, and more than one of them is acting suspiciously.

Miriam finally thinks she has discovered Jonas's secret.

Will Miriam grasp true love, or will it forever be just out of reach?

USA Today best-selling author, Ruth Hartzler, was a college professor of Biblical history and ancient languages. Now she writes faith-based romances, cozy mysteries, and archeological adventures.

Ruth Hartzler is best known for her Amish romances, which were inspired by her Anabaptist upbringing. When Ruth is not writing, she spends her time walking her dog and baking cakes for her adult children, all of whom have food allergies. Ruth also enjoys correcting grammar on shop signs when nobody is looking.

www.ruthhartzler.com

Made in United States
North Haven, CT
31 October 2023

43453311R00095